D1452698

NIGHT TRAIN

STUDIES IN AUSTRIAN LITERATURE, CULTURE AND THOUGHT

TRANSLATION SERIES

Friederike Mayröcker

NIGHT TRAIN

Translated and with an Afterword

by

Beth Bjorklund

Preface by Bodo Hell

ARIADNE PRESS

Translated from the German *Reise durch die Nacht*, ©Suhrkamp Verlag, Frankfurt am Main

Library of Congress Cataloging-in-Publication Data

Mayröcker, Friederike, 1924-
  [Reise durch die Nacht. English]
  Night Train / by Friederike Mayröcker ; translated and with an
afterword by Beth Bjorklund ; preface by Bodo Hell.
     p. cm. -- (Studies in Austrian literatue, culture, and
thought. Translation series)
  Translation of: Reise durch die Nacht.
  ISBN 0-929497-53-8
  I. Title. II. Series.
PT2625.A95R413 1992
833'.914--dc20

92-6497
CIP

Cover Design:
Art Director: George McGinnis; Designer: Itrice Sanders

Copyright ©1992
by Ariadne Press
270 Goins Court
Riverside, CA 92507

Preface

Bodo Hell

For readers who would like an invitation to the text, or for anyone who would rather read a short foreword than a long afterword, a few basic ideas and key terms; in retrospect, however, as well as in prospect, my remarks will appear to be lean, bloodless, and skeletal scribblings in light of the overwhelming wealth of sheer evocativeness in Friederike Mayröcker's mysterious masterwork.

HALLUCINATION/CALCULATION: The undivided text *Night Train* can be read both literally for its language (without, however, it thereby being a poem in the strict sense of the term) as well as discursively for its content (without, however, it thereby affording any comfortable recourse to traditional modes of narrative reception); the linguistic volubility is evident at every turn in the form of daring expressions that range from neologisms ("overbra") to unusual, even dual-language compounds as well as cross-overs and dream words ("air gal," "glacier butter," "momentary-stove bliss") and further to numerous misreadings and Freudian slips; such usage signals a verbal freestyle that brings together words—and thus also thoughts—for instance by alliteration ("hat/hound"), or identical rhyme ("bookmarks like lifemarks") or anagrammatically ("Goya Joga"); that serves to launch a calculated automatism of speech, leading to slips of the tongue and the eye—as if it were a matter of course!; in the most abbreviated fashion possible, two meanings are often collapsed into a single expression ("namely the wreathes/writers in front of my window," "only half an hour later you find yourself with your parrots/papers"), giving rise to multiple levels of semantic significance, as abundantly evident in the above examples; . . . it goes without saying that such forms of polysemy present nearly insoluble problems for the translator and that shifts in meaning are unavoidable; on the other hand, though, the translation offers the reader of the target language, in this case American English, the stimulus of a largely self-referential text that has, quite literally, been transported from one linguistic shore to another; . . . the seemingly ii

self-generating virtuoso flow of language is narratively punctu-
ated and rhythmically structured by a series of recurring
formulae ("repetitive mechanisms, hypnotic cycle, a principle of
repetition culled from life"); these litany-like expressions have
diverse functions: to relativize what has just been said ("what
should I call it," "who said that," "all of that is however only
conjecture") or to affirm a previous statement, albeit not always
unequivocally ("to tell the truth," "I saw it myself") or directly
to address someone outside the text, perhaps even the reader
("can you follow me," "understand if you can"); with such
seemingly simple ploys the author creates a repetitive pattern of
constant interruption,   while at the same time the reader is
periodically reminded of the context, as if he or she were suddenly hearing once more the clank of the train on its trip
through the text

KEY WORDS: "Neglect," "Fire wheel" (Verwahrlosung, Feuerrad)
The motif of misery rings out like the ostinato of a bass viol at
many points in the text; the mood of hopelessness and incon-
solability arises from the perception of physical jeopardy, the
aging   process,   and   the   disenfranchisement   of   the
female/gynandric I-figure ("I could easily neglect my external
appearance to the point of irrecognizability. . . never change my
sticky, soiled under and outer clothing. . . wear loose baggy
clothes. . . let my hair, which has become white, hang down in
long thin strands or shaved off down to my head". . . . "baffled
roaming woman, bag lady"); the imaginary existence of a tran-
sient presents a potentially lurking danger as well as a real-
istically envisioned counter-image to a form of existence that
would enable a woman to meet the demands of life and a career;
the imaginary existence is characterized by the adjective
verwahrlost (neglected), which is etymologically related to a
now-obsolete form, warlos in medieval German, "without
attention, protection, supervision, or unconscious"; that meaning
of the word wahr inheres in a positive sense in the modern word
wahrnehmen, meaning "to be aware of" or "to attend to" (which,
incidentally, has nothing to do with wahr meaning "true," as
opposed to "false"); the Verwahrlosung of the hermaphroditic
self designates a highly desirable form of productive un-
consciousness, allowing for the free-flow of energies that under

normal circumstances would be blocked by societal conventions;
. . . as an emblem of unbridled imagination, Friederike
Mayröcker employs her own version of a saintly symbol, the
"fire wheel"; occurring in other Mayröcker texts as well, the
image reminds one of St. Catherine of Alexandria (c.
310), who was condemned to be tortured on a burning wheel; the "fire
wheel" confers creative power for imaginative and verbal feats
of a superhuman nature; as the driving force behind the interior
life-generator, it guarantees the ultimate authorial desideratum,
the activity of writing

HUMAN BEING/ANIMAL SUBSTITUTIONS: as a concrete em-
bodiment of numinous presence, the hallucinatory text
sympathetically appropriates all living beings within its
associative range; it is thus not surprising to find an array of
hybrid forms, and the Mayröcker land-, sea-, and skyscape is
populated by totemic animals that serve as a heraldry of the
unconscious; at the positive pole of classical meaning there is
the "heavenly lamb," at the negative pole is the werewolf;
animals—domestic, wild, and those in captivity—function as
preconscious metaphors for states of being that are not
completely mute, but not yet verbal either; first and foremost is
the dog, the furtive double of the speaker ("they, big as well as
small, always look at me on the street as if I were in fact one
of them"); then there are the fox, lynx, wolf, and deer ("the
bafflement of the people when they see my HORNS, my
ANTLERS or the PROTRUSION ON MY FOREHEAD");
further, the camel, zebra, bat, gull, owl, cuckoo, crow, and
parrot ("upon emotional stimulation I try to endure this parrot
language")

NADA/NOTHING. THE TALK OF THE TOWN: that bold conceit,
as the original title of the work, reappears in a dramatic
rendition of the text that Friederike Mayröcker cast for the
Vienna Festival *Wiener Festwochen*) in 1991; the imaginary stage
of the surrealistic theater version presents figures familiar to the
public from *Night Train* (including the author-*I*, Julian, the
"Prompter," Lerch, the old couple in their rocking chairs, and
James and Susanna); it then seems completely natural that the
characters participate in the ostensibly nondeliberate, unself-

conscious incantation and conjuration that is known as "speaking in tongues," as conceived in either a religious or a psychopathological sense; and that gives truth to the expressed intention of the author: "every sentence should be a message"

Translated by Beth Bjorklund

We've now returned from France my PROMPTER and I and in the sleeping car I just saw the cold hanging meadows whisk by, with clouded eye because the night hours were tearful also damned and so forth.

In general the time there was not good and nothing worked out, least of all with each other since our relationship had exhausted itself; not with the course of events either which may be attributable to the circumstances we didn't know the language, still didn't despite numerous attempts for the longest time to learn it despite my love for it, and the whole time cursing thus cursingly through these three weeks and not understanding a thing of all that happened around us and finding everything very strange and restricting and threatening and constantly feeling unwelcome, indeed, a specter in the midst of this so imperious city in the midst of those clearly self-satisfied noisy inhabitants, everything up to the edge or somehow. While tears come to my eyes.

I always take one or two down pillows along on a trip because otherwise I can't sleep in a strange bed, and the one thing I learned on this trip was how to sleep any time any place, my body learned it even before my mind, my body comprehended it on this trip in these strange surroundings, something that I could never do before, a sudden inclination inspiration gift perhaps because I was tormented to such an extent, thus it rocked me to sleep last night in the travel bed, I slept above while JULIAN tried to sleep below, climbing up to the top bunk was not difficult, earlier I would never have been able to fall asleep there much less sleep through the night I mean in a night train like that racing through unlighted areas: for fear there would be a collision up front with the engine and all the cars, jumping the tracks, would tip over and bury their scantily clad passengers beneath them, and I cried until later in life, cried for my children growing up who died in that way, I say, *James and Susanna*. Thus I groped in the darkness for the brass-plated steel frame of the bed, my skull would in any case thereby be cracked open, and far from any shelter all my *dilapidated* things, my whole *dilapidated* body in which hardly anything seems to be in order anymore, that is, almost nothing functions anymore as it should, I say, and I constantly disregard it unless the pain prevents me from forming an idea or finding rest. I felt very inhibited about using the chamber pot during the night journey, the pot that stood next to the bottom bunk in a case with a latch on the outside, merely the thought of it made my bodily urge disappear in the distance, all of that is however only conjecture. . . and while my PROMPTER reprimanded me for having begun to talk about the weather namely the prevailing weather conditions and I asked him whether by virtue of his sensitivity to weather he could predict that it would remain as it had been, he for his part began to complain about the general condition of the world, then later he said it would be easier to bear if *everyone* perished, I wanted to ask more about current world conditions but that would have led too far afield: I noticed that by the lead weights, the ridges of my questions, in the folds of my gown, thus I held back, preferred to keep things to myself, the red-blindness is catching up with me, I say, questionable what kind of experience I could have gained if I had wanted to have the lens of a dog's eye implanted. . .

Intensifications in red, an excited, exciting color, a Spanish-red or Goya-red, a color that is not particularly becoming to me because it easily flips over into green, foists a green off on me, the flowering umbels on the windowsill, I slip into the shiny red velvet pants (Goya pants) in the morning, tears are already flowing, whereby I have so little red in my apartment and no red clothes either, once when I was very young I wore a tight red vest, presumably to emphasize my great height, while the fly nets bothered me, I say. Early this morning LERCH called me up and said *maja was girl, majo guy,* in regard to my recent question. Ramified resources! dwarfed, I mean, thus the Christmas laundry on bare knees. This marvelous color this red floods over me, these wonderful Goya-red pantaloons, I am literally dying to write in a hallucinatory style, I mean I need only to let myself go, I need only to close my eyes and let myself go, oh, how my blood surges, my veins. . . am I not rather a man, Goya is for example my father, am I perhaps my father, my own father, gilder of my father, or my mother, or am I perhaps my PROMPTER also called JULIAN and disaccustomed to any bright overly extravagant colors (soap), or am I perhaps that reddish-blond sleeping car attendant who superbly looks after us in every way on this our trip that never seems to end in exchange for an *excessively large tip* slipped to him immediately after our departure from Paris. . .

thanks to our nervous control system these two insights (inscapes) overlap, namely myriads, one fingers I mean feigns a story, thus one fabricates it, I say. And although I for example have myself sometimes become my PROMPTER he remains mysterious, hardly ever in all these years have I met anyone who remained such a mystery to me, strictly speaking he remains a total mystery, the painting with the nasturtium (Manet) captivated me, the subject matter knows no limits, the infinite painting is a propogation of life, a continual process of destruction and beginning again, we push heavenly love as upsilon down into the abyss, but each movement is important like the wind, old-fashioned I incline toward scalding, deafening, bleeding, although I have always enjoyed a particularly acute sense of hearing, I say, my auditory canals are sensitive like those of a young child, I often see children press their hands to their ears when there is a loud noise, night butterflies come like *tigers* into my room, the flaming angel is open in the man. . . and only half an hour later, says JULIAN, you find yourself with your *parrots / papers,* Our Lady of the Journey, I say, fatigue sat in my head and in my limbs and I shook it out by turning from side to side on the headrest, the shades up, Strasbourg in the dawn, a deserted athletic field, framed by whitely shining elder bushes, everything in my life was always garbled and blurred and blunted because there is always a flaw in the most beautiful heavenly pleasures devil now and again, thus I always tended to take a questioning, dependent position, and I tended to ask everyone for advice and enjoyed being instructed by anyone so that my view would become sharper, my opinion firmer, and as the light suddenly went out and my eyes were not useful for anything anymore no matter how wide I tried to open them in the midst of this nocturnal questioning, there still remained the consciousness of my body, my flesh, my thighs felt as usual to the touch, my aching feet, how comforting!, still able to carry my body, all sorts of things could be read from that, I say, all sorts of things for one's well-being could be deduced from that experience, I say, it was lightning outside—*what does outside mean?*

The chattering with oneself has also remained the same, that familiar blather, also what goes on within one's skull, etcetera, one's own sighing. . .

sweated out, now I have almost sweated out my life, I say, grope my way to the lavatory, look at my contorted gray face in the dull bathroom mirror, a worn-out gray in the mirror, my heartbeat resounds, echoes in me like claps of thunder, my children growing up, I would have bequeathed everything to them if they had lived, a garden the neglect of which often touches me deeply, you neglect yourself, you give in too much, my PROMPTER calls, but I don't go for that, the scene is always the same, the soul, at the writing desk, at the summer place, in the night, here in the night on this never-ending trip. How fortunate, one knows that the sun will rise in the morning, red, completely red, at Hochroterd I often exchanged letters with LERCH and picked bunches of flowers violet and white, today is Sunday, sometimes one doesn't know what day it is, it's a matter of color, it's a matter of tongue, the ara / parrot in the pet shop, with zebra stripes on its chest, with a knowing look, it looked at me a long time, it's a matter of the new color, it's a matter of the new tongue, the new look that / so that I can rest somewhere, take hold somewhere, that / so that my foot can somewhere get a grip, I mean I roam I only rove around, my nervous system is full of vibrating tensions, I want to do at least a dozen things at the same time, I can think, feel, understand, remember at least a dozen things all at the same time. When people hurt me I myself am guilty, I mean I take responsibility for it because I am guilty. Night butterflies like *tigers* in my room, the date pit in the middle of the room, on stork legs, the good day, my watch-glass window has awakened, the bold mountains fall on the beautiful sun, my work table stands close to the open window, presumably too close to prevent all my papers from being blown away by the slightest breeze, thus I have been in this room long enough, thus I have been in this time long enough, I have also become shy of the world, avoid meetings and contacts with people, my desire for quiet and elimination of every disturbance becomes increasingly great, has almost become greater than my desire for food and sleep, but I don't know what goal I thereby mean to pursue, it is as if I wanted to reflect on something but I don't know, or don't yet know, what it is, I have indeed undertaken everything possible, I have come in contact with countless people, have exchanged places and seasons, but in fact I have not moved from my place of writing, from my *writing*, naturally my place and my dwelling is here, but perhaps all of that only takes place in my mind, perhaps it is so that we live only in the illusion of doing this or that, perhaps we carry things out only in our minds, I say, possibly we live only by virtue of our power of imagination that we have cultivated and applied for decades, all of that is however only conjecture, I say, it's lightning outside, it's two thirty-four in the morning, the train has arrived at a station. Am I at home am I not traveling and on a trip, can I choose between a half-light, light, half-heavy, heavy hat (hound), do I have a choice between dark and lighter-colored clothing; if however I am traveling and on a trip everything becomes understandably more difficult, I am disaccustomed to any bright overly extravagant colors (soap), I mean for days I have been disaccustomed to soap, any use of soap, no bathing for days, which has not yet had any specific consequences, otherwise, at home, the best ideas occur to me during the process of bathing, several times a day, all in good time, so that the notebooks overflow from it, but here, I say, during this oppressive, hapless journey my body fluids have come to a standstill I mean I could probably remain so for days without the environment or I myself thereby having to suffer. Old-fashioned I incline toward bleeding, scalding, deafening, although I have always enjoyed a particularly acute sense of hearing, sometimes I was even able to generate an echo effect by what means I don't know, my father could do it too, that's a strong standpoint, all in good time, once my father took me (as a child) along to a church tower, while he rang the bell I ran through underneath, the clapper grazed my head, I could easily have been killed, when at the age of five I went on a hike in the mountains the boundless storm turned my umbrella and carried it away, *one could see the horns to the right and the left on my figure,* once when I was tending cattle an angry bull attacked me, the animal would have gotten the best of me if the hired man had not come by, but my mother called to my father as intercessor, she stammered prayers of thanks to my father that he had rescued me once again, like so many times before, my pipe-father, poor pipe-father, gilder of my father (Goya), NADA. NOTHING. On the back of the dog there was snow. . .

What happened to the lemon, I say, to the color yellow, what happened to the time, I say, where did it always go, how was it really, I say, how should how could one still find rest there or come to one's senses, my word in the blood gutter, suddenly something sprang from the table: things act on their own accord! two pieces of bread came to lie on the floor, presumably having fallen from the breakfast table, incarcerated between the windows a fly buzzes—I would probably have to free it, a mobile made of clothes hangers, an approximate distance to everything, a lemon lies on the table: *a beauty!* it lies there, I say, as if it wanted to prepare itself to be painted, and as my fingers clasp it I am reminded of something, it has to do with my father, everything basically has to do with my father, I hadn't thought about it for a long time, I say, all in good time, first that with the lemon, when I went to him he would sometimes make little things disappear in my coat pockets as a joke, apples, oranges, crumpled-up paper or small objects from the household, it made my pockets stick out, and only when I put on my coat to leave was I supposed to notice it. Embankment and shore, the shiny lemon lies there, next to it a red napkin, I say, he fell backwards in his chair, once he lay face down on the sofa and seemed to be sleeping, and I was frightened, doors and windows blown out (heart), thus I've been in this room for so long, thus I've been in my time for so long, thus I've long been listening to the footsteps of time above the people. . .

in the interest of truth, the felt pens ran out, blue and green in the night, big blots with jagged edges have flooded everything, ruined all my notes, when I was looking for shells yesterday I reflected on value and the absence of value, beauty and ugliness, the deception and seduction of the world, it was difficult for me to remain oriented, the subject matter is always unreal like the waves of the sea, I say, viewed retrospectively I've staggered from one disaster to another, charred and burned, almost tore out my eyes, cut my hand, often speared up the colors, hectic sugary things. . .

Table and desk, the small pencils, the alarm clock. . . why, I ask myself, can't I get rid of the maddening compulsion at times to drive a sharp object through my eardrum, I open my mouth wide and an enormous sun-eclipsing, raging angel in black-claw attire breaks open the two white snake eggs in my red-palate mountain range with its sharp wing blades, whereupon my revenge fills itself momentarily with a greedy tangled viper's brood that threatens to smother me so that I vomit blood. . . the many virtues, I saw it myself, the white cloud of flakes, I want to get lost. . . because I love them I often spear up the colors, but I have disaccustomed myself to any bright overly extravagant colors, but I become very excited when I see dark-red, dark-violet trees, flowers in the environment of my room, the beautiful letter with the parrot seal, the patterned ara in the window of the pet store for example, those are parakeets/parrots on the clothesline in the courtyard, yellow blue and green clothespins in the wind, a Spanish-red, Goya-red weasels over into green, upon emotional stimulation I try to endure this parrot language, in the northern part of the city I saw a street sign RUE OBERKAMPF, next to it HELP I LIVE in spray paint, notes against hail, also other hail and lightning rods, the heart should catch fire in the blood of the pigeon, after the lightning accident I repeatedly saw flashes of lightning before my eyes, I saw it myself how the car without a driver moved haltingly forward, the flier's cap the flier's May, the motorcycle helmet, the motorist's hat, I have various hypotheses about it, crying and writing, in a notebook, *perhaps also driving,* as I had noted down at night, he really loved to drive, was always a fast and ardent driver, my mother in the passenger seat, next to him, almost died of fear, I even have a photograph where she is racing along with fluttering hair, literally with a *fluttering head*, I saw it myself she sat with a silver sash on the running board of the Talbot, with an unfathomable smile on her sweet face, her hands clasped on her left hip, my memory does not go back very far, I can hardly remember anything at all from my childhood, my memories are preserved in old photographs, that's also the way I remember myself, I say, my father, all the deceased relatives and distant family members, certain movements of my body seemed to elicit blinding lightning flashes, I didn't remember them immediately upon awakening but rather later while doing some household task or another, oh I know the forehead is north, the feet south, the left arm west, the right arm east, oh I know the little monkey is waiting outside, fluffs up its coat, the little screech owl sat on the door mat and waited for me to let it in, while I sit inside, with my legs stretched out, until my feet smoke, the smoke was already rising, they were already singed, I say, I saw it all coming, she calls, I have often had such a premonition, I even dreamt about it, I don't remember exactly but everything seems to have to do with my mother, constricting coherence, everything seems to have to do with my mother, with my father, he is shrouded in beard and woods, I say, and he was a rock without compare / air icicle or when he wanted to tell me that he would like me to go for a walk with him and I used one of my perfidious excuses so as only not to comply with his wishes, such as: THERE'S NO WEATHER TODAY!, THE WEATHER IS SO TRANSITIONAL FROM COLD TO HOT, OR THE OTHER WAY AROUND!, I reproach myself, oh I reproach myself for my detestable maliciousness, my shameless unkindness pushed to extremes. . . pipe-father poor pipe-father, oh how much you loved life. . .

("Gianozzo, where do you live, little lamb? Can't you appear to me?")

Like a sacrifice like an owl, my heart is actually an owl, my bones are frightened. . . *I am already very light, alive* I have become accessible to everyone, I identify with everything around me, relate everything to me, *is it still because of my vanity?*

Life has withdrawn somewhat, has almost ended its performance, I made an analysis at twenty-five and at forty-five, broke off everything again, a cataract of tears, the pain in my stomach and heart contributed its share, actually the dream is gone, *I am so afraid of story-telling,* only notes, gypsy-like, marginal scribblings, or on old envelopes, JULIAN is colored green, his concerned gaze rests a long time on my face, but JULIAN is interwoven with rain and warmth, I mean the color pink, *or Beauty through Truth.* Thus a team of birds, for seven months seven years no seventeen years I took the opportunity and it proved to be right, but why can't I reveal anything to him anymore? I lie here, now I'm lying here, the soft raging in my breast, presumably swarms of birds. I lie here, with closed eyes, but the sounds of the outside world press through to me, I follow them with closed eyelids, become conscious of them, am able to decipher them. I open my eyes, prop myself up on my left side, can't focus anymore, close my eyes, it's still very early, I hear JULIAN climbing the stairs, to his room, he was doing something outside, presumably making breakfast, is now lying down again, like every morning. I lie here, now I'm lying here, it got me, inexplicable as most things that affect me. When I remain quiet the swarms of birds gradually settle down, as soon as I move however they fly up, as if startled they all fly up, in bad weather even the clouds, what do I know. One must remain quiet and not move in order to hold them in check, the doctor says, you are quite normal but one never knows what might come, I say to him, no it's nothing psychic, this time it doesn't have anything to do with my nervous system, this time it's somewhere else, chest, apparently the heart, what do I know, it wouldn't surprise me, I say, after all the excitement and stress and the trying circumstances of the past years and decades, it wouldn't surprise me, everything has to end sometime, but too soon, *it's too soon for me!,* I cry to my doctor, *I still have a lot to do!* How weak I feel! I lie quietly on the bed and wait for the end. At the same time I feel confident that everything could still change for the better, but moments later that seems doubtful again when I consider my condition. I also compare my situation to that of my father before he was brought to the hospital where he died a few days later, it's five years now, to the day, he calls me to him, but I don't want to go yet, I cry to my doctor, I don't want to go yet! Do you understand, can you follow me, I cry to him, this portioned-out life! this my portioned-out life and writing has done me in, through the decades it has completely done me in and ruined me, I don't even see so well, how weak my eyes have become, one can hardly judge anymore how vaguely one sees, one even gets used to seeing poorly, like everything else, a dry mouth, a taste of iron, what do I know, to tell the truth, I spent most of the time at the summer place with a senseless running around back and forth as if I were constantly in search of something, I ran upstairs to the upper rooms and down again without having found anything, thus the days passed, breathlessly, my whole foot is a stone, I gave as an answer when JULIAN asked me, is there a stone in your foot is there a stone in your shoe, shall we go for a walk? (he had his hand on the latch of the garden door), but I said to him, you know we've just come back, then he played the alpine pipe inside the house, I sat on the threshold between the living room and the porch, it was before or after the storm, the birds called loudly and hopped around in the tall birch trees, in the middle of the garden, two figures clad in white went past outside the garden on the edge of the meadow, bluish shadows, the bluish shadows, I say, the armpits my bluish shirt, and if one pauses a bit in the midst of the splendor, if one lingers a bit, one is momentarily admitted to this realm, caught up in the web of this PRIMEVAL MEADOW, in this population of hemlock and lady's smock, clover, elder and horsetail, chervil and nuthatch, speech-boy, poppy and rape, mosquitoes and butterflies, yarrow, caterpillars and salamanders, and how the women's hair grows in the blond fields, I call, I am perhaps on the edge of a body of water, when the wind blows through my reed-hair it's a flute tone, oh the hair of my children, smelled like nuts, or metal. . . *James and Susanna. . .*

In bent-down, *particularly in mountain regions* (remote), I saw the lyre assemble itself without transom from two bent tree ruins in the forest, also a freshly tarred road winding its way before me, above it a cabbage-white butterfly, while the evergreen forest raised and lowered its *conductor's hand* and commanded the sixteen winds so that it seemed the winds did not rule the forest but rather the forest the winds, it seemed also to hold them in the same rhythm. Thus the tall fir and spruce with their *vow and victory hands* in each gentle breeze, with their *vow and victory hands* waving upward, in contrast to which the leafy trees apparently preferred to remain an instrument of the wind, perhaps a gesture of rebellion, I call, or what did the evergreen trees want to tell me? My shadow appeared as an animal person, ugly hybrid being, thus I trudge through level woods, an aura of sanctity the boy in the garden in the rain with trumpet: rhubarb garden, next to the weeding father, yellow-green pelargonium. I woke up from the buzzing and razing of the scythe through the wet grass, amazing, from the whetting on the grindstone, it was still very early, loud hissing, and ski-slope train, the wreaked cars stood around sideways on the mown meadow, swarms of butterflies come past, when I lie in the garden or sit on the terrace, I follow them a long time, also wagtails, siskins, magpies, I see how they sway in the branches of the two birch trees, or from tree to tree, *I read a lot of Kafka.* (LERCH writes me about the author's stay at the medicinal baths at Riva), on the Holy Virgin's Day August fifth, I went the way of a cat and picked mugwort and valerian, *name comes into the nonpossessions.* . .

a time, I say, without compare, in which it goes from one weather condition to another, and we believe to be able to read the bodily state of the coming day on the traces of the wind, on the cloud formations and colors, on the depth of the shadows, once I also wanted to write the genealogy of my steps that carried, no, drove me lightly from the mountain over the meadows and paths toward the valley, *with the apostles and airplanes,* and how exhausted I was when I finally reached the valley, bouquets in sleep, I saw the scarlet-red pelargonium nodding in all the windows, or drops of blood (world-set). . .

also dream words, I call, red propeller-bow, momentary stove that warms the soul, one is more inclined to take a dream for reality than the other way around. Although there are also such moments! The gleaming harness in the flock of butterflies, I STILL SEE, sensitive immersion bath, I STILL SEE, LOVELY NATURE! the time has not yet run out entirely, I can still be an astonished witness, forest shadows, heart flights, poaching air. . .

a still life, standing still, breathing, nothing moves, moments of perfect happiness, a nature-memory, I say, it smells like burnt night, pine boughs, grave chamber -

in the interest of truth, I saw it myself, my furniture stacked high in the air to the last piece since the field there is not wide,

I again saw flashes of lightning in front of my eyes, or when a flash of lightning at dusk immerses the landscape once again in gleaming light, actually tears open and tears apart, thus I again saw flashes of *memory-lightning*, the truth is, I am a person almost without memories, I have for example only the most unclear memories of my early and later youth, but perhaps life has become too extensive to allow for an overview, I say, perhaps the motives are stored somewhere, but fog has moved in, the line of the horizon can no longer be made out. Everything too vague, here and there still points, recognizably clearer places that might offer clues to other fixed points, most of that is however merely conjecture, a shadowy something that momentarily seems to approach a tangible level of memory but disappears as soon as we attempt to grasp it, thus I could scarcely attain certainty, perhaps a waning of my mental powers, I call, thus the felt pens ran out, constricting coherence, it has to do with my father, everything has to do with my father, I am very weak now, it's three in the morning, my sleep is again interrupted, I lie on the top bunk, blue and green in the night, return trip from Paris, the felt pens run out then, flood all my notes, or what should I call it.

Blue and green waterfall, a stream of tears scarcely to be checked, my father is staying somehwere in a different time zone that we cannot reach I mean with our bodies, the boundless storm, I say, that hurls us into the immediate proximity of a condition of inner and outer *absolute nakedness,* defenseless nakedness of being born and dying -

("Gianozzo, where do you live, little lamb? Gianozzo, little lamb, do you want to graze on the sky? Can't you appear to me?"). . .

Thus we've already made progress in comprehending important things, I say, or moved to a daytime scene: *Beauty through Truth.*

In front of me green. Tears. Pine trees, weeds, shrubs. We don't weed we don't mow. Odor of burnt night, sometimes in summer a great sadness comes over me, a great anxiety, a great compassion for him. Pale sun, sweet moon: how much he loved all of that, warmth and mild air, and the swarms of butterflies. All of that flowed through him, all of that made him happy, it now flows through me, makes me happy too, I have become my father, gilder of my father, and it's already gone again. I stand at the window, a night with a full moon, I lean out the window, look at the moon the first three stars, draw in the fragrance of the linden trees. He stands next to me, close to my side, leans on the window like before, smiles, breathes, and is silent. Doors and windows blown out (heart), the pink blossoming in the garden. A shadow crossed my gaze like a razor, I'm very frightened, I cry about everything. On the table lay a peach seed, half a nut and a leaf from a cherry tree all of which I loved very much, I live now only in the left-over space in my room, today about seven o'clock I was what I really am for a moment, all of that is however only conjecture, I often ask myself is the suffering *in my soul?*

Life. Nothing. It becomes somewhat more difficult, long reflection, sudden recoil. Nothing. Long pause. Still nothing. God is in my heart (half a heart form), the hook below, the hold in God. Why always only half a heart? He doesn't leave me, even when other people do, everyone does, that depresses the flight, but he flies over walls and mountains, through the depths of the sea, and over the heights of the mountains, the lower part is an arm, a wing.

No one. But I saw someone on the street in nice clothes, bareness directly at the crown, webs between the fingers (knot of hair), leathery green moped driver as a salamander, his copper-colored helmet glowing in the evening sun, a boy with a skateboard under his arm came by, the spotted woodpeckers appear to me on the Holy Virgin's Day, I spear up the sun, I spear up the colors, from the Austrian landscape clothes, next to me swan and alpine pasture, closely related travel clothes, then I spear up the colors, two clouds (coats) namely the photos that I took of myself in the south villa (Espang, Allerheiligen). . . it was like a *sweat campaign, then he tore up some scratch paper outside,* and I felt it in my body as if someone tore apart my innards and heart, I am beyond help, where is my bee-like diligence, where did my bee-diligence go, where did my children, where did my baby teeth go, sometimes a beam of light through the drawn shade of the sleeping car, shameful condition of the body, I scream to myself, humiliating state of the body, vagabond-like travel clothes, I want to get lost, humiliating state of the body, I call, *as woman when one grows old as a woman,* I mean that is a more humiliating matter than when one grows old as a man. . . my miserable papier-mâché feet can hardly be felt anymore, my small leather tube: sagging body, *abandoned, I am principally groundless,* bareness directly at the crown, I say, namely my organs. Something must also have crept into my organ system, a fateful confusion, or I don't know how to say it. And that could not have happened overnight, no that must have been initiated and announced years, decades ago, but I never paid any attention to it, in general never to my body I mean in general I never paid attention to any warning signs and signals in my body because it always seemed to me a waste of time, my other energies have also receded, my mental faculties, for example, I forget everything, to tell the truth I have become a person without memories, I have literally forgotten everything that was ever important to me in my life, here and there it may still flash up in my mind, and I see the past go by in front of me, but I have forgotten most of it, actually everything, a few clear points remain, I say. Self-hate and self-shot, can you follow me?

My words fall out, my hair, I react only with embarrassed silence when I'm supposed to talk to someone, I've always been the opposite, throughout my entire life, the opposite of a competent *self-salesman,* even what I possessed in abundance I could never give thus communicate to anyone else. Not like those ingenious *self-salesmen* who over the years brazenly make capital from their feeble or nonexistent writerly talent by releasing the emanations of their wayward brains on the public, in contrast I've never had a knack for that, I've always, throughout my entire life, put myself in the background, I've never trod the streets of success, I've always made the biggest detours, not only in art but also in becoming a human being because I've never had a *gift of gab,* I call, because I've always felt myself so *outside the world,* I call, *outside all clouds,* namely mental block (filly-out), from the smaller letters, little pointing hands like phalli, shoulder blades of deer. . .

I spear up the colors, my papier-mâché feet don't function anymore, then I spear up the colors, in my dwelling (aviary) in front of my OLYMPIA (Manet) that has become old, but Goya had already painted his MAJA much earlier, I say, green, as

mentioned. Red. Now I'm almost gone, my life is already almost
over, but there at our *writers' residence* (summer place,
Allerheiligen Espang) I ran like crazy through the rooms and up
and down the stairs, namely because I had planned to let my
writing rest there I almost went crazy, my *writing* lay fallow
there, I had forbidden myself to continue *writing* there, and
instead of being able to pursue my *writing* I ran around for
hours, up and down the hills, and with racing pigeon steps this
way and that through the huge garden and constantly in circles
on the terrace, as long as my papier-mâché feet held out, but I
spent most of the time lying down reading, I spent most of the
time reading my favorite authors. The truth is, I never picked
up a book without pen and paper in hand, nor have I ever been
in a position to get involved with a book without constantly
taking notes, it's like a disease. It's also always been a criterion
of the quality of my reading material: namely where there was
nothing to write down there was also nothing for me to read
etcetera.

Place of insight. If a verbal idea has remained with me until
morning, a single sentence, if I have succeeded in formulating
a single sentence, if I have been able to write down a sentence,
a verbal idea, I fall on my knees and utter a prayer of thanks,
if I have succeeded in writing one sentence, a series of sentences, I fall on my knees, thank and pray, flow away in humble
prayers of thanksgiving, prayer fantasies, because I never believe
I can accomplish anything on my own, in my completely dilapidated inner and outer existence, I say, it's a miracle when my
writing is successful, at least parts of it; it's a parable, says
JULIAN and veils the sun with my black clothes, then they have
become your LIFE NOTES, says JULIAN, whereby he lets his
fingertips glide over my dusty furniture. There in Allerheiligen
Espang I didn't have the prerequisites for my *writing,* I call, I
mean it always drove me away and I always felt I had to be in
search of something but I didn't know what it was, perhaps my
writing grounds, writing abyss, which I find self-evident here at
home, but nowhere else.

The small pointed stones in the berries, the colorful hopping
birds in the crowns, I call, everything prayer fantasies, even the
breathing, this your breathing in the next room, I call, is already
confusing, a tenderly moving distraction, actually the dream is

gone, but when I'm with you at another place I don't want to be without this your familiar breathing next to me, although it basically challenges me to breathe in the same rhythm, but I can't do it, am not capable of it, although I'm very adaptable, have always been, indeed was brought up so, and to the extent that I let myself be dictated to I also react against it, which finally calls forth depression and pain for my own indivisibleness, a desired, a self-imposed enslavement, no, mourning, I call, but reacting, I call, can you follow me, a heart attack, a snake attack, all in good time, a pear leaf on the kitchen table, some people grant me only a phantom body, I'm afraid of writing, no, rather my salvation lies therein, I'm so afraid of failing, I'm afraid of story-telling, I'm against story-telling, have always been, I've always been against naked story-telling, perhaps because of its disproportionately large claim, I say, I've never liked the large claims on the part of my surroundings either, if I meet someone with large claims I immediately withdraw into myself, I withdraw into the farthest corner, it appears to me like another *obligation,* in the same way *unbridled: stung,* can you follow me, do I not have eight arms and can do a lot of work all at the same time, think a lot? Thus far my life has been a matter of revealing and exposing, my writing in contrast a matter of concealing and distorting, but now the techniques are reversed, or aligned with each other, how should I say it, I'd like to be relieved of acting, or: I'd like to be relieved of any action, or: I'd like to forestall any attempt at action, or: I'd like to avoid any acting and any action, there are indeed parallels, I say, I'm hardly capable of acting and I'm hardly capable of allowing an action, I don't like to act and I don't like to read anything that has action, thus neither do I write anything that has action or could suggest it I mean it blows my mind, the dominant part of the soul.

My chest explodes when I think about it. . . there in Allerheiligen Espang, there I suffered a complete *decline of words,* I felt myself declining, I'm declining, I too am declining, I had only the books to thank that I did not really perish, I say, perhaps I had really developed into a shadow figure already in those days and weeks and months, at this our *summer place,* the suspicion came to me, that when people who crossed my path no longer made moves to avoid me they actually wanted to *go through me,* all in good time, but then at the last minute they finally did make way, as when one makes way for an outrageous obstacle on the sidewalk, excrement of dogs for example with obvious displeasure and repulsion, that's a strong standpoint, I say, I went the way of a cat and picked mugwort and valerian, for the most part I didn't understood anything of the stories that were told to me, that's it, I don't understand any of it at all, to tell the truth, I don't understand anything or anyone, a garden table, the typewriter on it, a couch, a wobbly stool, a wastepaper basket, that's my writing position, my living position, nature smells like burnt night, or down the stairs to a childhood home that was once my most familiar place, *and it's already gone again.*

The green knights come into my room at night, through the small open window, grasshoppers, rose beetles, iridescent night butterflies, the blueness of the morning incomprehensible, I hopping and squatting at the pond, following the rivulets of the stream, pale sun and sweet moon in the sensitive immersion bath, rose-colored afternoon hours, swarms of butterflies. . .

I was always obsessed in many directions, I inclined toward obsession, from the beginning, does it however befit us to be or to seem absolute, when we are in truth only weaklings in matters of love. . . addicted to love and art, addicted to art and nature, milieu was also handwork, or how should I say it, the small pointed stones in the berries, the colorful birds calling in the thin crowns, sometimes I don't know what day it is, but I let time run forwards and backwards, for example I never start to read a book without pen and paper in hand, and, to tell the truth, I fall on my knees when I have succeeded in writing a few pages, I cross myself before a trip and beseech God for his blessing on me, and a deep feeling of pleasure flows through me when I can use my legs my feet as before, how swiftly, how nimbly, how thirsty for knowledge they run before me, they even go up hills, without delay I want to graze on the sky, I trudge through level woods, voice of the rain or antlers, moved to a daytime scene, *when I included Parma,* I say, *when I brought up Parma, but in an erroneous connection,* I mean when I told about a reading I had held in Parma but forgot that it was in Italy not France, I mean I told about my trip to France and then right away about my trip to Italy, and I always got the cities mixed up, the Italian with the French and the French with the Italian, only in the case of Venice was I sure, I knew we were there in the rain and the hotel was inhospitable because it wasn't heated and I walked with head down plunged into the stream or whirl of people, thus with pounding heart and carrying a large umbrella I went for a walk in Venice on all five days during which it rained almost continually, and with pounding heart over the busiest bridges and overcrowded streets and plazas, occupied with fending off the idea that people passing by or coming toward me could come too close to me with their umbrellas and might injure me, thus I constantly feared the worst, strictly speaking I couldn't think of anything else, the truth is, I saw nothing of Venice other than open umbrellas and the threatening approach of passers-by, so that finally I literally invited an eye injury, indeed called it down upon me, especially the young people put me in a state of panic anxiety when they came toward me with their open umbrellas or pushed against me from behind, I felt constantly threatened, was constantly bathed in sweat, made way finally for even the glance of those coming toward me, *death through the lions.*

Threat of bared teeth, violent!

I saw it myself, namely on all those trips, Italy, France, and always a different city, I say, a greater open-mindedness is present there, a greater unity but also the most unrestrained noise, then my jawbone broke in two I mean from all that noisy confusion my jawbone broke and generally everything, the strong friction between the soul and the outside world, I haven't been able to live with myself anymore for a long time, and everything gets away from me, then I fly down and up, together with my mother, all of that was then very wearing, sometimes I thought I was destroyed but then finally something entirely new came out of it after all, can you follow me, that's a strong standpoint, I want to get lost. That saws open my veins, makes my blood clot, ties up my abdomen, breaks open my breast, crumples my heart, dismantles my face, strictly speaking I'm a monster and totally out of place, don't fit in anywhere, I mean I roam I only rove around, find myself in a deplorable condition, purely externally, these insane productions internally, I fly down and up again, first down then up, together with my mother, we take off from the windowsill, watch out for the high voltage wires, actually the dream is gone, place of insight. But I have thereby gotten to know the uttermost element, but there are the fire-feet in my dwelling, I say, a gust of wind, rumblings outside, the muslin billows up at the window, on the mound, in the wooded heights, from the window the willow trees hung with tassles, feathered weeping willows, washed-out green, *what then will become of me when I die when I am dead,* crumpled-up heart, the crows in different directions, how you read me!

Snowed with blossoms, at that time, the rods of the trees in the pale evening light, the mighty elder trees with enormous blossoming monstrances, in a courtyard, a child crying softly in the distance, the swallows singing in the faded rectangle of the sky, invisible warbling blackbirds: everything of unearthly origin, I say, as if I could have gotten a conception of it at that time, a conception of it in those moments of deepest stillness, how the memory of this image would consolingly accompany me away *when it becomes imminent.* Polly says however that time will reverse itself, parts of us can already grasp it, that is also the reason our past is at the same time our future. Tomorrow: Thursday, the week divides itself again, I imagine in regard to my dwelling a deep relationship or what should I say, the musk gifts in the morning, the finger brushing, oh partly overcast days: don't seem to go away!

The string-nine in the rivulet, the bloody-brown sun in the morning, work of the subconscious I'm often surprised how many associative flashes can light up in my head simultaneously, fireworks as it were, a system of electrical sparks, if only our actions like our thoughts could be as fast as lightning! What Polly claimed recently was totally untrue, namely that fantasy and potency diminish after the age of fifty, precisely the opposite, besides the fact that the power of association increases rather than decreases with increasing age, later Rosalia (September 4th). I read that book throughout the winter, also took it along to South Tyrol in March and always put an old postcard from LERCH in it as a bookmark, isn't it strange, I call, his card travels along everywhere, the reading has already become easier, but *I must still be very careful not to become fully involved with the book and finally disappear in it altogether. . .*

greetings to you Maria Ebensee, dream-end, there the entire terrible sun flashes directly on my optic nerve from the rearview

mirror of a parked motocycle, I was blind for a long time, now
I am also forgetting how to write by hand, I say, imagine that,
I say, I can hardly write anything by hand anymore, except for
those scribblings in my notebook, *those ingenious ideas,* I say,
which I can't even decipher when I find them again after a few
days, now for example I have literally forgotten how to write a
letter by hand, then I fall into making a formless mechanical
gesture, a shapeless scrawl, thus *depravity of the head,* I say, or
mental laziness, particular characters of the alphabet also turn
out oversized, others shakily distorted, one notices also that the
lines were written with great effort, thus I've lost not only the
ability of thinking and combining but also that of writing by
hand. Now after the memories have almost totally gotten lost,
I've also lost the ability to write by hand, brain branches
beautiful entwinings, gradually I forget everything, I say, gradually everything seems to fill up with things that hinder my
writing if not make it entirely impossible, all of that is however
only conjecture, in the sun-speckled countryside, we're just
crossing the border, the idea occurs to me that I am on the
verge of losing the consciousness that I gained decades ago of
being an adult, those are strange connections and coincidences,
I say, I had mastered it at one time, I say, but now I am again
the astonished obedient credulous (old) child, which at my
advanced age is naturally neither notable nor desirable but rather
appears only as ridiculous and repulsive, thus I am beyond help
regardless of place, regardless of situation, only half an hour
later, says JULIAN, you find yourself with your *parrots/papers*
and no more thought of the pain, *life must really be totally
demolished before we can find ourselves!*—Sometimes it comes
over me like a terrifying idea, I call, what would have become
of me if for some reason I'd had to remain *illiterate,* in what
abysses of forlornness and despair I would then have been
thrust, one can picture all sorts of things, I have however perhaps been saved, I say, at least at times, a *manuscript* decorated
with jewelry and brothers, on the *typewriter. . .* and the
yellowing grass between the stones, today the lampshade covers
up the nearly full gleaming moon when I move my head a bit
while lying and reading, I almost began to laugh about it,
imagined animated animating dreams, pigeon plumage, fell
asleep again, giant palm groves formed a dome in front of my

eyes, namely the back armor of giant turtles jutted up out of high horsetail woods. . .

depraved as I find myself to be, I live only in the left-over space in my room, I say, everywhere in my *dwelling* the newspapers tied in bundles, books and papers, an inconceivable mess, all of which I'm still going to read, I plan to anyway, Japanese-like pictures and goblets, brain branches, tender entwinings, gradually everything here fills up with things that cannot possibly be beneficial to my *writing,* indeed hinder my *writing* if not call it into question, all of that is however only conjecture, I say, and I look at the pieces of glass on the parquet floor, a glass fell to the floor, in carelessness I had knocked a glass from the table, my fingers are already bleeding. I also find myself repeatedly confronted with the possibility of a partial or total loss of speech, I say, I often feel the need to tell someone about my mental fantasies, to inspire someone with them, or how should I say it. I also think sometimes how comforting it was during those summer months with a self-imposed writing prohibition to find the same feelings of misery in the works of my favorite author, I wouldn't have been able to read anything else in those days and weeks and months of depravity, I wouldn't have wanted to read anything else as I lay there and suffered the whole time, *someday I must find a way out, or at least reflect on the course of the matter,* otherwise everything would indeed have been in vain, can you read me?

I have brought you the Discomforter and so forth, says JULIAN and looks at me meaningfully, I press him, who or what is the Discomforter, does he or it possess human form? I'm very confused, can't get a hold of myself, he's sitting across from me in his travel clothes, he presumably plans to leave me, smiles down at me mildly, I'm very dependent on him at such moments, entirely without dignity, I regret nothing, I leaned on him, didn't keep my head, a kind of absence of consciousness frightens me, soon now comes the big reckoning, I say, LERCH too always used to sit in front of me like that, I was never able to keep him, he came and went as he saw fit, the conversations came and went between us, but something was lurking behind the conversations, it seems to me today, it was like a flying and falling, yet there was something concealed behind that perhaps my secret wishes and his secret defense, I say, in the smaller

letters, I say, I would have liked to address him always with
DEAR LITERATE, he was a music thinker, polyglott, actually
the dream is gone, sometimes it seemed to me as if we were
being observed, as if someone were listening to us, all of that
made me somewhat euphoric, even the thinking about him.
JULIAN crumples an empty cigarette pack, smiles thereby in
satisfaction, everything somehow illusory, I call, everything only
empty crumpled days, I call, everything done wrong, everything
wrong, it's all only lies, I call, everything a lie! it's fake the
way people talk and move and look at each other and act, it's
all only lies, everything a lie, one's entire past as well, everything wrong, it's all a fraud, a sham, oh if only I could do it
over again!

And a person doesn't want to be confronted with one's own
past at all, I say, when one has reached a certain age, as I have,
as we have, one doesn't want to have to look back at all, since
everything was such a disgrace, one single disgrace and hypocri-
sy and forlornness, thus a past in the face of which one can
oneself only be horrified, I could do without my past, but most
of all I would like to begin again, the truth is, one doesn't know
until later, probably too late, that one has done everything
wrong, thus one constantly wants to wash oneself clean, to begin
anew, perhaps it's a dream of humanity to realize itself in that
way. . . a single shoe on the sidewalk, two men disappear into
a driveway with a long roll of linoleum on their shoulders, a
heart attack, a snake attack, the snake-like dark winding
branches of the tree of the gods, in front of a background of the
morning sky glowing with marvelous bluish-rose colored light,
the blood-red lacquer blossoms, amaryllis (knight star), flowers
of the night, quickly quickly before I start to cry. . .

And no more looking out the rear window of the moving
train, I call, we have bought ourselves free, we give birth now
from our heads, in the interest of truth, cracks in reality, the
view of the holy proportions behind it, snowed with
blooming. . . an echoing bark in my ear, rapid writing, in a
lenten cloud, there are indeed very different levels of reality,
thus I burn with desire, *this sky-and-sea-roaring sofa (obsession)*,
thus I am new each day, the little monkey / the little lamb the
little screech owl wait outside, our lost children, I call, our
descendants! and went out already in the early morning, through

the glistening meadows everything so lush my God, and only to get rid of the stuff that morning in the midst of the blooming waving splendor, in the sparkling mountains at that time, our first summer together whether you still remember? a rapport! an impetuous angry love was in us at that time. . . my head is so white. I look down at myself, see myself lying there clothed, he's only building a doll on the table, inversions of the use of the body. *Then he tears up some scratch paper outside,* but I feel it as pain in my whole body, as if someone were tearing apart my innards and heart, an uneasiness, a feeling of wretchedness overcomes me at that moment and again I feel the swarms of birds flying up in my chest, I feel the fire wheel. The car in the meadow stood there with its obliquely-parked left front wheel as if it wanted to swing out, actually to swarm out, first the sun on my back, now it shines in my eyes from the right, also freezing, icy in the hoarfrost, thus I lie there, covered over. With an old glasses frame, worn-out clothes, loose footwear, in the shabby room, and in the morning the warm rain when I went out of the house briefly, the larks above the stubble fields, the herbage the lakes full of mirrors and swans, three fire salamanders crawled across my path and in front of my feet one after another, they moved forward laboriously, when I bent down to them they feigned dead, the good day, I shrivel up, I too die, the distraction in my feelings, when I all too carelessly went out simply to do a small errand, mail a letter, JULIAN wanted to hold me back by calling, *in that outfit!—in those clothes!*—for the most part I passed it off laughingly, with a simple smoothing out of my clothes I could make everything reasonably acceptable again for my immediate surroundings, or the image that I never perceived but imagined with pleasant feelings, as JULIAN, standing behind me, helps me with my coat, turns up my coat collar because he knows I like to have it that way, gently places the thin overly-long strands of hair over it, as if he were dealing with a child's head of curls, I've always imagined a type of eternity, the neck lined with a lace collar, the lace collar turned up over the coat collar, my thin hair over that. . . oh numbing phase of life in which everything comes together, comes together in a single melancholy moment, I say, perhaps my memory will return then, I say, perhaps that which left me so long ago will return, I've become a person without memories, my memories have somehow gotten lost, I say, I don't know how that could have happened, perhaps because I've let my life pass by like a dream, thus everything faded away just as dreams fade away, this midday light that floods the street in late September, I call, it makes me the happiest person for a moment, I call, the beautiful seeing, from old horse marches, juniper gardens. . . houses walking on stilts. . . I saw it myself, it changed the nature of my *writing*. . . a remarkable network of string, a string-nine on the edge of the street, thus the eyes hoarfrost-struck, fields, and open mounds, the last larks above the stubble fields, the flickering half-shadows in the sky, shadings of a stiffening earth, a beautiful and difficult drawing, the firewood that was piled up around the small windows of some houses almost completely closed up the front side, it looked like a fur-trimmed, beardy-wrapped form, in such disguises, or models, the high trees on the avenue in gold and flames, also single poplars. . . and that with the mushrooms, I say, drags behind me like a tow, I say, he was well-versed in mushrooms, widely traveled, a music thinker, think helper, thought chronicler, I'm talking about LERCH, and our love had been a harmony that redeemed all else, a unity that resolved everything, *uttermost element!*

All of that makes me somewhat euphoric also the thinking about him, thinking about LERCH and how it was between us at the time, but my notes only imagine things, not all of it is true, or I only invented it, so that it's often hard to say where JULIAN STOPS and LERCH BEGINS, or the other way around, the two figures sometimes seem to be connected, their delimitations uncertain. All of that becomes clear to me finally this morning, has become so transparent, tonsure of the trees now, from the window, only sparse foliage on the lower branches, as if I had to squeeze a small hard lemon I tried to empty myself. . . while traveling around, I say, I read three books, I read in three books at the same time, while traveling around I attempted to transfer the passages I liked to my notebooks, soon then it belonged only to me, I mean I had the feeling of having written everything myself that I copied, actually I like best of all to read in glossaries, I looked for what I liked and I found the books that kept me alive, one referred me to another, one led me further to the next one, I always followed my own inclinations, in the interest of truth. The same textual passages, read in different moods, can move one to tears as well as leave one cold, I say, that means perhaps a hunch that sun and stars also rule here, also one's daily disposition, which at any one time is composed of innumerable and imponderable elements of mood and feeling, determines the form of a text to be written, or something must necessarily become a poem when it possesses the predisposition for it, or how do you deal with it?

Beauty through Truth, it is the abyss that encourages me, upon emotional stimulation I try to endure this parrot language, or as LERCH used to say, very respectfully yours, in trance (Honolulu). . . doors and windows blown out (heart). . . in the night from the 27th to the 28th, Goethe's birthday later Rosalia, September 4th, mere description does not do it, here is a different style, *detailed passages namely as melancholic woman*, the little phalli in my room, shoulder blades of deer, godmother Leipzig, the dogs bark on the horizon. . .

something haunts me, pursues me, comes over me, suddenly I see the blond child again, Frankfurt airport, under the quince tree, October 9th, I again feel a desire in my fingers to cut a lock of hair from the beautiful blond boy, he smiles over at me, all of that is however only conjecture, I say, the involuntary batting of an eyelash, all of that happens in such a way that we hardly notice anything, I mean we are not hindered in seeing, I lie in the sleeping car, sit here at my desk, in my dilapidated dwelling, all of that finally becomes clear to me, all of that is so mixed up, I have refused to believe in many things, I mean I roam, I only rove around, the sleeping car attendant greets me repeatedly and with conspicuous courtesy every time I look for the bathroom at night, I scurry noiselessly up and down in my oversized plastic sandals, am startled by my face in the mirror, make faces alone in front of the mirror, utter soft laughing cries, that meshes in my head thus complexly suspicious words, I like to imagine things, I like to carry things out in my mind, wish for actions as fast as lightning, such as I have become accustomed to in thinking, otherwise everything literally gets stuck in wishing, I say, otherwise we carry things out only in our minds, how for example will something edible appear on the table today, I ask myself in the morning, it goes through my head on my way to the post office, a blond hairstyle in the

window, the butterflies like tigers who said that, you must ask
the good Lord about that, calls JULIAN, you should control
yourself more, keep things to yourself, I for example prefer to
keep my problems to myself, says JULIAN, otherwise anybody
could come and *want to sympathize* with me, a detestable
conception, then I would also have to take into account the
feelings of the other person, he would only aggravate my
condition, I would in that way only lose time, he would then
make claims on my time by occupying himself with my
problems, transfer his own feelings to me, measure his moods
by those of mine, compare his own existential agony with that
of mine, by what means I don't know. . . thus tangled up in
thorny bushes, I say, I saw it myself, gray-starring roof plumage,
houses walking on stilts, I was caught up in various delusions. . . on the back of the dog there was snow. . . I often
seemed to myself to be indifferent toward good and bad, I
avoided participating in the events of the day, I noticed at times
not without consternation my complete lack of relation to the
world, but I had always avoided quarrels and controversial situations, but I spear up the colors, am disaccustomed to any bright
overly extravagant colors, I am deeply moved when I see dark
red, dark violet flowers, look back again and again in order to
let this passionate color affect me once more. . . oh if only my
children had lived, a garden the neglect of which often touches
me deeply, you neglect yourself, you give in too much, calls
JULIAN my lamp-lighter, but I don't go for that, in love with
this article of clothing, with this worn-out coat, says JULIAN,
you are in love with this article of clothing, but it doesn't
become you, isn't really becoming to you, says JULIAN, a sudden inspiration, in love with this article of clothing, with this
coat, because you attach to it your hope of being able to secure
for yourself in that way a carefreeness in life that is otherwise
reserved for one's youth, a devastating situation gray-green
crumpled, *an overload, an overkill, an overrun coat!,* furthermore
backpack and gym shoes although those years are long gone for
you. . . what happened to the time, I ask, where did the time
go? from day to day a decreasing ability to adjust, a faster rate
of exhaustion, and the consciousness of continuity seems to have
gotten lost. Thus Assyrian with pearl necklace and beard, I call,
fluttering clothes on a summer evening. . .

and the anger of the lamb is certain. . .
after the storm, the birds called loudly and hopped around
in the tall birch trees, in the middle of the garden, two figures
clad in white went past slowly outside the garden, on the edge
of the meadow, carefree, says JULIAN, easygoing, brain aviary,
your life seems to be marked by a certain carelessness, your
mistakes and dislikes in thought and feeling stem from that, your
states of anxiety, your false reactions: always afraid of losing
something, or missing something, an occasion, an object, parts
of consciousness, remainders of your memory, you are even
afraid of losing your *art of writing,* of perishing finally by
impoverishment of language, also you often seem to me to be
in a dream, sleeping and silent, responding only to your own
impulses, abandoned to your own thoughts. . . and you ask yourself increasingly often how you would act if something life-
threatening, restricting, and strident, some *serious event* occurred,
and how you would deal with such distress . . .
the crown white, all of that proceeded haphazardly, *meanwhile he had to wait,* a wild bramble bush grew out of my
mouth, often I hear the Danube too, as if the pure tone had
called the wind that blows today. . . while the racing train
almost hurls me out of my bed, on a curve, on this never-
ending night journey, it's ridiculous: morning toiletry! everything
must finally and definitely be cast off, these crazy *shopping trips*
which always end up with a person feeling forced to buy things
one basically doesn't need, records, books, suits, hats, scarves,
clothes, and household appliances, whatever, accumulate, pile up,
lie around until everything falls to dust, until finally in the sixth,
seventh decade of life one believes to know what one has
always needed: namely not to want anything more and not to
need anything more, nothing more of any of that, to drag around
in the oldest rags, and in general, to the last torn-up focus, to
the last sleepless focus, with the burning wheel in my chest, fire
wheel every morning, the truth is, I call, I could just as well
give in to my dilapidated state, indeed that would be only fitting
and beneficial for my most ruthless *writing mania,* I could easily
neglect my external appearance to the point of irrecognizability,
by by-passing the morning toiletry for example, to the point of
torn-up because sleepless focus and the decision, never again to
change my sticky, soiled under and outer clothing, it became

increasingly clear to me, I already get along with only the fewest things, the fewest people, wear loose baggy clothes, old gym shoes, sailor hat, and backpack, let my hair which has become white hang down in long thin strands or shaved off down to my head, etcetera.

To tell the truth, I was indeed no pleasant sight, and my surroundings thanked me for it in their way, also my hair was falling out again, thus I became visibly unkempt, and JULIAN said, *you let yourself go, in your writing mania you let yourself go too much!,* no joint, I call, I don't need that, never needed it, euphoria even without the stuff, I call, complicated nature my watch-glass window has awakened (cognitive system), with the burning wheel in my chest, fire wheel every morning, flogged torn apart in the thorny bushes, odor of burnt night, baffled roaming woman, bag lady, somewhat euphoric and completely shorn, obsessed ravaged marked by a soft raving mania, thus numbing LIFE OUTLINE, enclosed in my fairy-tale dreams or on the other side of the street, rapidly changing associations: deer above the path, like me. . .

I'm afraid of story-telling, I'm afraid of the fire wheel in my chest, I'm afraid of the ill-tempered looks of the people on the street, old as well as young, who repel by attracting me and attract by repelling me so that I have to stare at them continually, without really wanting to, *of all the people in the world I am basically interested in only one person and that's me,* can you follow me, my whole life long I was always afraid, blinding, deafening, crippling, loss of language, airplane crash, death on the street, earthquake whatever, I search for truth but truth conceals itself, I am ignorant an entirely ignorant person, can you comprehend what it means to be an entirely ignorant person, you with your enviable unfathomable body of knowledge! sometimes you try to comfort me by professing that it is not necessary to know a lot and that you yourself don't know enough or: the world is boring, not worth investigating. But it depends on the friction between our souls and the outside world, always only on that, I call, like in the movie, I call, I saw that movie, that outrageous Russian movie, took notes, my gaze glued to the screen, without looking at the note pad in my lap, everything that I especially noticed and liked about the German version, inconceivable outrageous things, I call, I indeed have eight arms

and can do a lot of work all at the same time, think a lot. . . . I began this book on November 7th and began again the horse, hair and nails also nose of the ship, beard—everything of mine grows and falls away again, the dishes and the tail of horses decorated with turquoise, also cut artichokes, according to heavenly rules, I say, I'm completely wrapped up in my work but work cannot always be a support, all of that becomes clear to me this morning, has become so transparent, like the moon or something, I saw it myself, houses walking on stilts, the front side of which appeared full-bearded or overgrown, their narrow windows framed by firewood piled high and glowing in brownish-yellow fur-like colors, violin key of a woman, or automatically-operated machine for taking notes, I say, that takes notes in shorthand on everything that is said, at STALKER'S for example, I say, there I took notes on everything, the note pad in my lap, my eyes glued to the screen, I took notes on everything, thus wrote down the German version almost completely, I call, can you follow me, I was beside myself and overwhelmed, I call, I've hardly ever come across anything like that before, it becomes clear to me, makes sense to me, I liked it, I mean it made sense to me in a particular way, he's just building a doll on the table, or things have suddenly taken on a telekinetic mobility of their own. And my eyes remained fixed, remained fixed on everything as is my nature, I say, they didn't linger long and were driven further, lingered again and so forth always, something that you basically reject and dismiss because you are a so-called UNIFIED PERSON, straight as an arrow a ONE-WAY MAN, the hollow root and box trees, now I don't find any comfort. A numbing multi-faceted game, and hardly had I emptied the shovel-full of dirt into the open ditch covered with branches that then blew up and back at me, than I saw how Polly bent over it with a pale tear-stained face, and picked up remnants of fresh green that lay around on the gravel path along the avenue from the last tree cutting, she buried her face in them, then took more of them and thus came toward me. . .
pipe-father, something cried in me, poor pipe-father. . .
    now I don't find any comfort, boughs being placed, I call, the open grave, the burial chamber decorated with fresh boughs, I call, I turned the child's shovel, was beside myself, could hardly bear the gaze of the funeral guests standing in a half

circle around the grave, my gaze then fell on Polly, and how she with a tear-stained face reached for the box-tree branches and took them and pressed them to her, and for a moment I had the feeling again of standing in front of a mirror, in which could be seen the face of my father that bore my own features. . .

constricting coherence, I sense the odor of the underbrush, am I perhaps a man Goya is for example my father, am I perhaps my father, or my mother—*name comes into the nonpossessions*. I see mirrored in me what he was, and I see him now in me, I see his mirror image when I look at myself, look inside myself, I am so near to him, I am so similar to him, I become increasingly similar to him; it's no different with my mother, I become increasingly similar to her, I become increasingly similar to all the people I love, sometimes I see a double of him, run after him then, call to the stranger, smile at him. . . he used to stop walking when he started to talk, suddenly, even in the middle of a street, for inexplicable reasons, I say, it made me impatient and nervous, and I often tried to get him to go further by not stopping myself, most of the time then he just barely escaped a car by leaping to the other side of the street, in retrospect I reproach myself, make the severest reproaches, through this fault of mine he could have gotten into a dangerous situation, he loved to talk while walking although it was a strain for him, he was a reticent person, like me, basically a reticent person but he loved to stop while walking with his arms crossed on his back and talk to someone, to stop suddenly, in the middle of a conversation, presumably to direct the attention of the conversation partner exclusively to what he was saying just then, most of the time however when he stood still and started to explain something to me, I simply went two or three steps farther without concerning myself about him, then he seemed hurt, stayed back a bit, later started walking again intentionally more slowly, let me feel his disgruntlement. I regretted having hurt his feelings and gave him increased attention and affection the next time we came together, it was a beautiful *cooking* day in September, I say, a boundless storm, an approximate distance to everything, I saw the she-wolf in a dream, she was similar to me, *water-clear Alaska especially the eyes,* on the back of the animal there was snow, we went with the she-wolf in the dream to a cemetery, JULIAN and I, there he called me again, the crown white, he told me he wanted to take me to him soon, thus at the anniversary, I was very alarmed, the she-wolf glowing ashes, it was an open cemetery of medium size, the animal went ahead, turned around then however and toward us as if to make sure we were following, something had led us straight to this cemetery, the so-called PROTESTANT CEMETERY, one of my relatives was buried there, we walked through the rows as if we wanted to look for the grave of the relative, perhaps she, the long-dead one, had called us to come here, NACHTMANN, I read on a gravestone, STILLHEIM, LUISE V. BERG, SAPHIR, ULMENAU, SCHÖNWETTER, FINKHOF, LAUERBACH, PROMPTER. . .

. . . an unusual, arousing list of inscriptions, I call in the dream, then we walk farther through the cemetery grounds, until we come to a promenade. . . sit down in the cemetery then presumably in front of our common grave I don't know, the sandy ground in front of us strewn with fir needles, the cross to the south, branches of the fir, Scots pine, and larch hanging down to us, a blackbird warbles also yellowhammer siskin, and I see how the foliage of the leafy trees that stand here and there and tower above the evergreens cast their shadows on the gravel path mixed with needles, shaky arabesque-like shadows, from maple and beech and linden, presently I recognize the ivy-covered office building of the cemetery that was not visible before, flagged with the state colors, oak, fir, and Scots pine, tree of life, behind the building and connected to it the cemetery nursery, from whose gable a yellow cross blows, the mountain ash not nearly ripe, a pair of crossed hammers as coat of arms, wild cherries toward the sky, red beech, old lilacs, still a long time before the end of summer, a gingo tree blows gray undersides of the leaves, finally a sudden darkness that comes over the entire visible sky, also *gilder of my father*, "then you have a different ground under your feet. . . ," my hair is white, I was no longer talkative, but the she-wolf was nowhere to be seen, greetings to you Maria Ebensee, *the Christ Child in his upper body*, it echoes in me. . . colored green to an extent, but I go there repeatedly because of a garden matter, I say, I mean, I repeatedly intend to dream about it, in general certain dreams repeat themselves, I dream for example again and again that I have lost something, handbag, key chain, identification papers, but I can also order dreams, I say, figures in the belly of the ship and the body of the mother—I adapted myself to everything so as not to be conspicuous, I always dream about it, clothes for example, I adapt my clothes to my surroundings so that no one can recognize me from a distance, but also my mode of speech, I adjust my mode of speech to my surroundings, or my style of letters, some people grant me only a phantom body, I say, or my doctor advises me to pay attention to my health, it would be good for you to have a garden, says my doctor, go swimming! At least go for a long walk every day, says my doctor, but how, I call almost angrily, how am I supposed to build those two or three hours into my plan for the day, can you tell me that, I say, I have a small suitcase in the attic, in it I keep my bathing cap, swim suit, beach towel, and bath shoes, in early spring I take the things down in order to have them at hand at any time, but in late fall I bring them back up, without having used them, the small suitcase is black and bears the label SWIMMING EQUIPMENT, but it's been like that every year, I say, that I took the things down, that they only stood around here at my place for the whole summer, because I was never able to find the three or four hours to go somewhere and go swimming, and when the cool days come, every year the same thing, I bring the small suitcase, without having opened it, back to the other things stored in the attic, then I look out of one of the open hatches for a while at the roofs and church towers below me with a strange feeling of yearning and sadness, and toward the mountains on the horizon; in the half-circle above the silhouettes of the chimneys, half-circle shaped salvo, sheaves of blood-red ice-blue beams of light shoot up in the westward sky. . .

Basically I've let my life pass by like a dream, I say, basically I've done everything wrong, I say, basically everything has remained patchwork, my life, my relationship to the world, everything wrong it's all only lies, basically everything was a lie one single lie, what I said before, what I heard before, my notes only imagine things, none of that is true, or I only invented it, I take it all back, or I retract everything, everything a fraud, I call, also with love everything only a fraud, everything a sham, everything made up, everything recycled, reeled off, played out in all variations, and the anger of the lamb is certain—

also my notes, I call, are not the result of particularly profound trains of thought but rather literary techniques that exceed that which I myself can comprehend, and so forth, agent between father and mother, or a god-winter. I become increasingly similar to them, I say, a phenomenon, if I compare my smile in this picture with that of theirs in the mirror, a tuft of white hair hangs down over her forehead, the eyes shadowed, here as there, I become increasingly similar to her, I become increasingly similar to both of them, I often assume their form in my imagination, I often assume the form of my father, I become increasingly similar to him, I become increasingly similar to both of my parents, and because we have become so similar to one another, I can expect from them, and they from me, only the eternally same stories, I mean we continually tell each other the same stories, which has made us into boring people, most of all for each other, I say, and has a paralyzing effect on my mental powers namely on my written thoughts, or something like that, I want to get lost, but death in any case dissolves all connections, I say, until we are finally broken, that BASTARD DEATH actually manages to pull it off, and thus we are torn out of all connections, everything is finished for us, done and gone! in such disguises, or model, and it's already gone again. John the Baptist for example was able to choose his hour of death, dig his own grave, I don't see any advantage in that, he climbed in and lay down as if going to sleep, but no one knows where his remains are. . . *who among us has looked into the heart of a father?*

That's a strong standpoint, I say, I'm traveling again in a train, in dream, am naked, fail to get off at the right time, or I in my bareness avoid putting myself together and getting up, doing anything that would draw the attention of the other passengers to me, I sit huddled together in a corner, cross my arms in front of my chest and have pulled in my legs, some circumstance or another however then leads me to get off anyway but with an open umbrella, *one of those Majas?,* I've forgotten parts of my luggage on the train or left them there out of embarrassment? or I didn't find time to gather them together, I dream sometimes in that regard I could get my things together quickly, but so haphazardly that backpack and bag could hardly hold everything, I scratch myself bloody, I have to be able to forget myself completely in my *writing,* every night, I scratch myself bloody, my legs, my neck, perhaps as substitute I get off the train unclothed with an open umbrella, I saw it somewhere, presumably in Goya, I imagine myself then as a Goya figure, first with open umbrella, *one of those Majas* swerve to the left decidedly coquette which doesn't particularly suit me, later as one of his wretched shadowy figures. . . matted hairy cur, my body small wop, leather hose shrivels up, wretched doll's skin, *milieu was also handwork,* I say, can you follow me?

can't sleep any more, the night seems endless, now it's three-thirty in the morning, I'm very weak, ardently wish for the end of this night journey, I hold my breath, I bury my nails in my skin—

perhaps crutches, substitute, feverishly I start to read again in several of my favorite books, I switch on the small light, the second third of the night already over, thank God, and if it weren't so cold here I'd get up and go out and ask the reddish-blond sleeping car attendant whether he could heat a cup of milk for me and let me sit in his warm compartment for a while and look at him silently, at his table or sofa, *in that gear,* calls JULIAN, he doesn't say *suit* or *outfit* as usual but rather *gear,* he pronounces the word with a strange undertone, you can't go out in that *gear,* for hours you sit on your bed in that *gear,* even go out in the hall probably only to bother the sleeping car attendant, what will people think!, with that he had touched a sore point, perhaps even the sorest point, I can't stop brooding, I call, as it is I can't stop imagining what people think about me, I always see myself from the outside, with the eyes of other people, only rarely do I succeed in freeing myself from that, also from the idea of the oppressive presence of the other, I would like to find out what they think of me, and what they take me to be, why they despise me, ridicule, scorn, or the very worst, why they at times completely overlook, entirely ignore me, indeed *look through* me, sometimes it seems to me they could even *go through* me. . . I should of course be completely indifferent to all of that, and I've already learned a lot in that regard but not everything, and there are always relapses, the harness. For although I've already shaken off many things, something of a sense of shame or reserve still remains, BASIS WHERE EVERYTHING COMES TOGETHER, I call, and although I go out on the street in my worst worn-out clothes, I still avoid making a repulsive impression in any way, thus I would never have wanted to appear in public with my shirt open or a zipper open in my pants, or with a bare head without this my wig that I wear when I go out and which mercifully covers my thin growth of hair. But perhaps now I should always go to bed with gloves on so that I don't scratch myself bloody in sleep, while I sleep, I call, enclosed in my fairy-tale dreams or on the other side of the street the rapidly changing associations like deer above the path, I haven't always lived so abstinently as now, but I've always sensed a certain inclination for it, I scratch myself bloody, scratch myself bloody again tonight, imagine everything possible to avoid it, I like to imagine things, see myself suddenly as a Goya figure, *one of those Majas,* I call, open umbrella, swerve to the left decidedly coquette, that doesn't particularly suit me, then preferably one of those tortured shadowy figures, I say, sensations of the eye, when I suddenly step out of the darkness into the light, when I suddenly step out of a dark room into the light of day, my eyes are slow to accommodate, crossed-out passages, for example, with LERCH, threat of bared teeth again.

There are no witnesses, I call, but it's true I mean I perhaps dreamt it like everything else, everything with LERCH and the others, we often exchanged bones, stations like flugelhorns, mere landscape conjectures when I momentarily lift the curtain and look out, an organ tone when I breathe like the moon or something, ecstatic topos, this LERCH (or WALDMEISTER) had a face like MILK AND BLOOD or as said in fairy tales, and he had so much to tell, I sat leaning over his table or sofa the whole night, and he began a long way back, went from one digression to another, but my eyes remained fixed on him, a further instance, can you follow me? but, how far the desire drove me, I don't know, I had presumably only lost sight of him, and now he appeared again, and again I yearned for him passionately, I would have liked it, but he didn't seem willing, thus we talked a long time, I sat leaning over his table or sofa the whole night, my heart pounded wildly, thistle and heather in the paper grass we lay there a long time, finally his ear pressed to my breast to follow my heart beat. . . scattered straw, I call, MILK AND BLOOD, an open grave, and suddenly I also lost

blood, suddenly I noticed the pool in which I lay and began to
cry out of shame and fright, saw then how he turned away and
looked out the open window, the spring tide in my room again
now which I haven't left for days and weeks, I'm just a person
in a room but someday I must find a way out, or at least recognize the course of the matter, try to make it out, otherwise I'll
croak like an animal, buck or kid, the nanny goat accepted me
as buck and also as her kid, nuzzled my cheek, brushed off
clumps of hair on me, all of that is however only conjecture, I
call, little colored milking animals, I say, I wait longingly for
the next delivery. . .

that was rather much for the first time with the airplane, I
call, the jet cruised whitely in the vault of the heavens, and then
I hear myself crying dreadfully through the echoing subway
shafts, my underjacket sweaty, short alpine jacket, odor of
incense, thus I felt myself transplanted with the help of my
mental obsession, thus I felt myself lifted into the air, but soon
my skull strikes against the concrete ceiling of this dungeon
again, with the chair saints, I call, emerged from the waters of
sleep with the knife between my teeth, I call, flotsam and jetsam
of the night, or like the gypsies, I call, when they roast the raw
green beans over the open fire, while a shot is fired in the
distance. . . descent of the fire, and tingling of the chandelier!

I get rid of the refuse, time and again get rid of the refuse,
in this my completely dilapidated CHAOTIC HOUSEHOLD,
how many cleanings (removals) are necessary until we no longer
need to be ashamed of an essence. . . I don't know what cools
my wounds, it could be the all-penetrating and helpful power of
language, descent of the fire, thus it was lightning in front of
my eyes, I call, when I turn from one side to the other in my
bed in the dark, thus it was lightning in front of my eyes and
it all depends. In the photograph of me you perhaps notice a
similarity with the she-wolf I mean you perhaps recognize a
similarity between her smile and mine (lightning of the eyes),
lynx—

I'd like to be relieved of acting, or: I'd like to be relieved
of any action, or: I'd like to forestall any attempt at action, or:
I'd like to avoid any acting and any action, there are indeed
parallels, I say, I'm hardly capable of acting and I'm hardly
capable of allowing an action, I don't like to act and I don't

like to read anything that has action, thus neither do I write anything that has action or could suggest it I mean it blows my mind, the dominant part of the soul. . .

. . . to tell the truth I'm afraid of dying and I put up a fight against dying, I've always imagined a type of eternity, the neck lined with a lace collar, the lace collar turned up over the coat collar, my thin hair over that. . . oh numbing phase of life in which everything comes together, comes together in a single melancholy moment, perhaps my memory will then return in a flash, I say, perhaps that which left me so long ago will return I've become a person without memories, but then everything will presumably appear before me in a single moment, scarcely comprehensible in its alarming fullness and everything perhaps intertwined, descent of the fire, I call, agonizing remainder of life, and network of string. . .

not unbutton anything, I say, simply pull things down over it, short-cut procedure, everywhere, here, also the refuse simply in a corner, dripping water faucet, faulty window frames, ruined limbs, and I don't want you to talk again of a SEASON, of a WINTER SEASON when All Souls' Day is hardly past and don't want you to make plans for the coming year/blathering. . . who knows perhaps already my last! this entire broken-down world instead of like before spherically flattened at its poles, this whole dried-up dung, heart dung, rabbit lying down, this rabbit lying on its side, out of clay, in my notes/cards/just so they don't blow away! it's ridiculous! how seriously I still take all of that, still, still haven't learned anything from all that happens around me—

but still, just barely, just barely a recognition of the world, on oil paper, so it seems, just barely. Red on yellow, from the oil paper the tarnished view of the world, beaten world! and DELUSION! You are all too loud, you are too loud, restrain your feelings! downstroke and upstroke, scratching on an old slate, or as bag lady, paranoid woman roaming the streets, the vests layered-over, buttoned together, the rags in the morning for example, with bad breath, disheveled skull, wind-blown skull what do I know, sometimes bald, everything so far, so far away, to be with someone for example, oh so far away hardly imaginable anymore, to be with someone again, even the memory washes away in the last minute, sinks into itself,

withdraws, deadly orgasm brain aviary, the watchman has given up, the emotions from earlier swelling up and down
don't concern him anymore, are no longer of interest, swerve to the left, original feminine legacy, it's ridiculous, or the zebra finches, trouser fly, masculine swerve to the left, on which side of the trouser fly does he keep IT, on which side does he fold IT up?

Everything that flashes up, just barely still flashes up from the past, *and it's already gone again:* on the orange-colored sofa, under the bird string, the most passionate times with LERCH, LERCH'S clothes strewn on the floor, the crystalline winter air on his bare skin, LERCH'S clothing disguises, continuous consuming glow. . . everything concealed everything covered up long ago, everything veiled, running water faucet, oh my shabby body in its casing that has also become shabby, now, have found shelter in one of the old horse stalls, sleep on the ground strewn with potsherds, waste paper, kitchen refuse, I curse the cramped conditions of my resting place, hardly am I away however for more than ten hours but I feel the urge to come back here again, I hesitate to use the words *come home* in this connection, flash photo. Thus I wander around aimlessly, arbitrarily, everything long gone, over with, remoteness, juniper paths, mourning in the white moon, or something like that, as delicate as the topic may be.

in the interest of truth, I make faces at myself, threat of bared teeth again, violent, I am not certain in matters of faith, still not certain, although it would be high time for it. A strange shelter that hardly lets in the world, I call, underground, the forest in the mountain almost above it, everything in counter-light, everything untouched except the posts with the wire netting, the fat white cat as visitor in the mornings and the birds, then amazement again. An approximate distance to everything, the dazzling storm.—Running water faucet, I hear the water faucet in our sleeping compartment, I am very weak now, two paragraphs here, three pages of a book there, and if I like what I read then I want to have written it myself, I long to have written it myself, I mean I insist upon having written everything myself, thus I delude myself, I like to delude myself, and I let anything be done to me, I always prefer to let things be done to me, I say, at that time with LERCH (or WALDMEISTER), he pressed his ear to my left breast, he listened to my breast and counted my heartbeats and I let him do it, and he said as he carefully arose from my bed, *you let things be done to you,* how rightly he understood me, at that time, and I understood his words as a caress, only retrospectively did I discern a different meaning in them, I thought about it a long time, until I found something like an affectionate reprimand in it, later the flattering suspicion occurred to me also, he wanted to give my life a new direction. The many books, I call, we for the most part read the same books, each had his or her own copy, the most recent book by Jacques Derrida for example, about which we then also talked on the phone, I call, we often had long phone conversations about the books we were currently reading, we read the same books at the same time and we exchanged ideas about them, I call, LERCH and I, and we carried on long conversations about them I mean we exchanged *thoughts about reading,* we exchanged our *thoughts about reading* often in long conversations on the phone, presumably a mere excuse to hear the other person's voice, I say, I here and he there, and I soon noticed that he was able to grasp the inner connections better than I, indeed that he was in a position to endow them with delicate perspectival motifs from his own life so that they—on the basis of his body of knowledge that always received fresh nourishment—reflected the image of the world for him each day anew, bringing the idea of truth ever more absolutely before his eyes.

Love. Unrestrained passion, we were fanned by the coolness of the forest and darkness, with the chair saints / counter-instep, in the common harness, sun in one's head, momentary-stove bliss/long pause, tufts of hair between my fingers, I don't know anymore what day it is, my eyes remained fixed. Morning sparkle outside, everything full of allusions, playing and squinting or how should I say it, everything late too late, suddenly the desire to revise everything, in these my advanced years to revise everything, now for the first time to begin the *final version of my life,* or whatever. The scene, soul is always the same, everything dipped in the color violet, and highly smudged concealed in a lenten cloud this spectre this gushing sun-eye, thus read called into the ear, pleasing colors, but I am too conscientious, I was reared that way, I learned it well because my youth was not easy, etcetera, *actually I was brought up to be a person conscious of duty* that was however not detrimental to my *writing,* on the contrary, all of that is however only conjecture, my notes only imagine things, or I only invented it, a tongue-singing, ragged, tattered change of life, obsessive, fearful, embarrassing feeding as with animals, that fevers in my head from morning till night, BASIS WHERE EVERYTHING COMES TOGETHER, or what should I call it. To be able to begin again now, my God in my thirty-third year for example, then when we saw each other for the first time! The truth is that we often got into a stalemate in later years, didn't know in from out, gloated over the weaknesses that became apparent in the other. And if our children had lived, *then now at our age we would not have to love each other instead of a child—*

only piecemeal am I in a position to live, only piecemeal am I in a position to read, nor do I know where it will take me, what I'm supposed to think of it all, I feel disoriented, also indifferent toward everything that goes on, I can't organize anything in my head anymore, can't retain anything, everything dissolves, vanishes, I sense confusion namely disunity and fear, an utmost discontent, depravity, can you follow me?

sometimes I'm afraid that soon it won't be possible for me anymore to react to people and to the world, I catch myself sometimes trying to think, without finding an answer, what reaction would be appropriate in this or that situation, often I actually wait for someone to come to my help, to whisper something to me, *to prescribe and suggest my reactions,* so that I can then nod my head in satisfaction and can say yes!, a disease it seems: I constantly buy books for which I don't have room anymore at my place, sometimes I live as if there were only reading and taking notes. . . at that time, at our summer place I was afraid that the supply of books would be exhausted, a thought that threatened existence, I call, not to have enough books at my disposal. . . at that time at our summer place, Espang Allerheiligen, I fearfully dreaded the day when the supply would be exhausted, my heart sank at the thought of what I would then be supposed to read, after I had *finished reading all of these my favorite books to the end and finished taking notes from them:* this I announce: this my reading and

taking notes, I announce only this, this one last comfort, with
this I can forget almost everything else, everything intrusive and
infamous, everything beastly, everything offensive about the
world of people. . .

In my *mental world*, in this my *mental world* there seems
however to be nothing but standpoints and counter-standpoints,
I mean I take a certain standpoint and immediately I feel compelled to take a counter-standpoint, thus I waver continually
between above and below, far and near, center and periphery.

Thus I like to delude myself, I delude myself, there are no
witnesses but it's true, everything has to do with my father,
everything has to do also with my daily disposition, or when I
say the ecstasy decreases with increasing daylight, or one's daily
disposition, which at any one time is composed of innumerable
and imponderable elements of mood and feeling, determines the
form of a text to be written, or something must necessarily
become a poem, or a prose text, when it possesses the predisposition for it, *thus Beauty through Truth*, running water faucet,
like the moon or something, I looked for everything I liked and
I found the books that kept me alive, namely the abyss that
encourages me, sometimes I hung one of my favorite books
opened to an arbitrary page above my desk so that I could read
something from it, while writing, I mean so that it would bless
me, while writing, or how should I say it. . . upon emotional
stimulation I try to endure this parrot language, my eyes have
become weak, how long will it still be possible, how long will
I still be able to continue my *writing,* I'm afraid I always delude
myself about a lot of things, sometimes I think I delude myself
about everything, this writing and morning sparkle, the work
lamp with nurse's cap: scribbled-up paper, crossed-out passages
for example, how my blood *surges* today, my veins, thus I am
today for example very excessive and omniscent, all of that
makes me euphoric today, *thus the musical part of the blood
seems to be designed,* I say, can you follow me. . . my oval
delusion, ovally-drawn head rests obliquely on my raised
shoulders, a manuscript decorated with jewelry and brothers,
some people grant me only a phantom body, I call, we've
always known each other, since time immemorial, we've always
known each other, I call, oh we've known each other forever,
how wonderfully, how well we know each other, how intimately

we touch each other with our eyes, we stand as it were on facing balconies and wave to each other continually, over the geraniums that nod in the gentle breeze, I was then very excessive in my squandering and extravagance toward people, in my surrender to the side of the world, and I suddenly felt so well thereby, in my submission to people, submission would suit me, I call, in general everything, I mean I would finally have reconciled myself to everything, also to the most inconceivable life situations. In travel clothes and before she had to depart, she kissed his feet in her initial devotion, I call, and he accepted her gesture of submission, I call, my mother has likewise always been a submissive person *and* an entirely independent person, I mean a being with entirely her own drives and thoughts and ideas, *servile nature and free spirit in one*, exactly like me. That proliferates, I call, like a leg-of-mutton sleeve in the mirror, that escalates, gets out of hand, hardly comes to a standstill, that was a lot for the first time with the airplane, I call, do you remember, like walking tours and theater visits, I call, implicit delirium, sea- or soul-landscape, thus I attached myself to this my LERCH (or WALDMEISTER), at first hesitatingly then increasingly determinedly, years later when there was absolutely no more reason for it anymore I always still looked for him, years, decades later I always still played back what had happened, unrolled everything hundreds and thousands of times before my inner eye, tested my feelings anew during these situations that were repeatedly conjured up, and realized that they had become worn through the course of time, they had become vaguer, had receded into the distance, and gradually I saw us in my mind's eye as in fact only pale elongated shadows passing by. . . can you follow me. . . he more than anyone else was admittedly able to exert a sensitive indeed beneficial and refined influence which all his friends, even the more distant ones, eventually succumbed to, so that his entire circle of friends seemed to reflect him, if I perchance ran into one of them something seemed to remind me immediately of LERCH, be it that they were of similarly effervescent mental powers, be it that they had acquired a loving gentleness in dealing with people and things, be it that they were ready to be of help at any time. Some of them however, especially the women, achieved only a kind of outward similarity, they merely assumed one or another

characteristic stance, tilted their heads to the side while they
listened, or their eyes sparkled when one talked with them about
things they liked, and as much as all of that had been able to
send me into rapture about LERCH, it displeased me in their
imitation and emulation, indeed at times the entire group of
friends appeared to me as only his creation, the whole lot
deplorable in their efforts, and in that they acted like poor
imitations of the original they seemed to want to misuse and
diminish the prototype in my view.

Voice of the rain, or antlers, I call, I want to get lost, I'm
just a person in a room, I live now only in the left-over space
in a room, and always these problems! I searched for truth for
a long time but truth conceals itself, someday I must find a way
out, or at least recognize the course of the matter—

quickly quickly before I start to cry. . . I sit in my
seclusion, corrugated iron hut, there's a storm outside in front
of the window, my floor lamp with the nurse's cap, I've drawn
back the curtains a bit, which were earlier of a delicate ivory
color, now blackish gray, the waning moon, it always comes so
late at this time of year, if one travels at night one sees it
hanging above lonely valleys, or between the mountain peaks,
when everyone is asleep, in a monoglottal mode, a type of
flying, etcetera, discovered today the first signs of aging on the
back of my hands, I don't use very much of my furniture anymore, the Blessed Virgin of the Pillar, a table, two chairs, an
oven, sixty candles, in the specialty cabinet! thus concoctions. . .
let's galopp toward winter!

Rapid writing, I call, in a connecting passage, intense feeling
of fondness for sweets, I call, in a mood for nonstop nibbling,
tasting, trying a bit, or tripping with guarded step into the next
room to the open box of candy burgeoning with white lace
paper, *a mental gift!*: but now and then it demands also a stricter
etching, scratching, scratching to pieces, seclusion. . . concealed
truths, the pink light when I wake up in the night, look out the
window, steaming halo, closed moon (aura) in the room, *then it
hangs on one side like a clock. . .* I wear white feet at present
(sea gulls), everything animal compositions I don't know, are we
camels or lambs, do we fly to the sleep trees? and everything a
diversion, a disturbing distraction, I am not certain in matters of
faith, I can hardly think straight anymore, although I have rolled

out the visual field, neurotic forehead eye (overbra), to see and hear with all eyes and ears, I see better what I also hear, and vice versa, can you follow me. . .

but sometimes the ascetic life is too much for me, I'm tired of it, I'm tired of the asceticism of the past weeks and months, actually I've striven for it since my youth, and also lived it, with intermissions, through the years decades, the lips the moon curtailed. . . a pale flash of lightning in the white water. . . when a leaf falls from a tree the world trembles, I'm afraid, I'm also afraid, I've always been afraid, I fold up all too easily in front of people, I feel inferior, one fear replaces another, I say, my self-awareness is almost extinguished, a progressive deterioration becomes visible, indeed I'm hardly in a position anymore to meet friends or even the most intimate associates without timidity and inhibitions, without feelings of inferiority, insecurity and fear, everything has become difficult, everything has become inscrutable, everything has lost some of its effect, I'm hardly master of myself anymore, a constant distance to everything, a constant indifferent distance to oneself, observing oneself, condemning oneself have made life sheer agony for me, a sudden darkness that comes over the entire sky, I'm also not certain in matters of faith

How easily how unexpectedly love flips over into its opposite as one says, I withdrew for weeks, indeed months and was inaccessible even for my closest friends, didn't call on the phone anymore, didn't pay attention to the ringing of the doorbell, refrained from emptying the mail box, all in good time, I call, everything was taken literally, *I mean everything became literary,* but it didn't always prove to be a rescue operation. . . if I had initially counted the time of my suffering in hours and days, it was soon weeks, indeed months that had to pass before I was able and willing to surface again, if I had initially reckoned with only a few days, it had in the meantime become several weeks, indeed months in which I couldn't leave the house, finally didn't want to anymore either, I had as it were forgotten how to make contact with the outside world, indeed *to relate to the outside world,* I was really afraid of going out of the house, of going out on the street, of crossing the street, of going into a store to express my wishes. I was virtually paralyzed, I couldn't articulate properly anymore, as if I had lost my command of language, the sounds sommersaulted in an alarming way, people had trouble understanding me, starred at me because they couldn't or didn't want to understand, treated me like a mentally ill person, or simply left me standing, as if they wanted to give me time to come back to myself, to organize my thoughts: I felt embarrassed and angry, was close to tears, ran away. . . if it had initially seemed to be only a temporary illness, weeks and even months had passed in the meantime and the suffering had still not completely abated; if it had initially been only a matter of days in which he, LERCH, didn't call, it had become weeks, indeed months, so that I had to assume that his withdrawal was final, I asked the doctor whether my illness was merely of an *imaginary nature,* do you think, I ask my doctor, that I am suffering merely from an *imaginary illness,* does it possibly have to do with the waning moon, the waning moon hurts and weakens a person, perhaps because we believe the light has left us, I've been writing letters now for days, indeed weeks because so many thin voices call me, call away namely the wreathes / writers in front of my window, also rain-writers, scribes. . . through practice and reflection, claiming the land of our imagination especially in the morning when a condition of half-dream still envelopes us, but for you there is in any case only the ONE TRACK, calls JULIAN and sits up in his bed, only the ONE TRACK nothing else, and any distraction is only harmful, only the ONE TRACK of your thoughts is useful for you, ears in the store window. . . I also miss the train, I call, I don't have any time anymore, I miss my train and time gets away from me, I call, I don't have any time anymore, I don't have any time at all anymore, I mean I have never had so little time as in these years, I have increasingly less time at my disposal, earlier I also never had enough time but it was not so oppressive as now, I'm also very late *in this my time, and writing,* the works in front of the model always faulty, I also avoided removing the rough diagram after-wards, if a person is not settled down, nothing works out. In order for words, word patterns to be able to *arise* at all, a SOLITUDE is necessary precisely the astral spandrel, I did it with my entire physical being, in my pygamas behind the window, for years they came, this year they didn't, the colorful iridescent pair of birds, peeping and nodding, a remarkable

curiosity came over them as soon as they saw me. I often talked
to them, sometimes they tried to fly in, they landed on the
windowsill and wanted to come right to me, I chased them away
at once with gentle though insistent words, and they seemed to
listen but not want to understand, for hardly had I left the room
for a short time but they again sat on the windowsill, preparing
for a flight into the interior. . . those misunderstood appearances
of color, I call, those galloping illnesses, intensifications in red,
that little black-haired girl, propeller-bow in her hair, a deep-
red pink wavered on it, the hem of the coat bunches up and
drags on the ground, in fright when a person is frightened these
panicky crashes into the depths, I fell down deep for a moment,
then one seems to perceive the surroundings as if in a magnifying glass, to regard its virtually obtrusive insignificance as
bitter scorn, the hem of the coat bunches up and brushes the
ground, I no longer notice my shoulder bag / red patent-leather
bag, we had suddenly lost sight of each other in the underground passages of the subway: completely distraught I observed
the untouched unmoved repelling faces that surrounded me, one
of my constantly recurring nightmares, I say, after a certain
point however they seemed to reflect my state of fright, little by
little I sank into a strange hot embarrassed brooding, a stranger
to myself, transported to an indifferent distance, suddenly I saw
the victory angel of the Bastille in front of me again, flooded in
light, shooting upward into the light-blue evening sky, saw again
the hand of the director of the institute, as he, while I watched
with great interest, picked up a French magazine to cover a
large-size photograph of a prominent writer that was lying on
his desk, felt again the strange desire to devour small round
objects, the small French coins for example had done it to me,
I call, I had the desire to put everything into my mouth and
swallow, the cap of the felt pen, the small spherical travel clock
that looked like a piece of chocolate candy, the little balls of
crumpled waste paper, I see now the purple skull of the sun
behind the afternoon clouds, appearing and disappearing,
depending. Now the purple skull has disappeared behind the
clouds, or a bird call that strikes one's ear, however not only
the letter U is round but also the mouth that speaks it, *the
flaming angel is open in the man.* . . can be a pearl in my life,
but perhaps the photo is only so scratched up, torn off, worn

thin: as if I were sitting in a flaming *bus* with four other people, the second from the right with the bow-tie / beard, who smiles triumphantly because he is in flames, reminds me a little of pictures of my father in his youth, I say, *this recourse namely course of speech,* as if one had trimmed his nostrils, eyelids, ear lobes with a small scissors, thus worn out and torn up, I saw it myself sometimes in the morning I already wear the face of my old age, right away then I want to get it trimmed, cut, cut to size, that's a strong standpoint. Namely as Kleist is supposed to have said upon viewing a painting by Caspar David Friedrich ("Monk by the Sea") AS IF A PERSON'S EYES WERE CUT OUT. . .

I sit up, in the semi-darkness, something whistles past my left eye, November crows cross the picture from right and left, sometimes in the night when I get up, when I stay up a long time until the wee hours of the morning and leave the light on so that the birds outside in the barren garden are deceived and think it is already day and begin to sing, at my window, I say, thus in my velvet beret, flier's hat, children's apron what do I know then everything comes as easily as children's shoes then everything fits easily together. At that time and drawn toward it, I blew the alpine pipe made of alderwood and fell on my knees, fell on my knees the very first thing in the morning and stammered a prayer! in the threefold whirl and echo, *hurling out and everything!,* driven out of me like beads of sweat, oh this confectionary profession: I went in for sugar, was also set on fire! The black-violet heather around our thatched-roofed house is veiled in hoarfrost, now the eaves are broken, black-gray fields, like burned-up coal / love—then sudden rain. Went in for sugar white like in the morning light, EACH OF THE CHRISTIAN WORLDS WHITE LIKE A CHRIST, etcetera, thus all sorts of dreamt things come to mind, I say, or I was caught up in various delusions, my arm got into an odd twisted position while I was sleeping, had become numb by the time I woke up, last night I was seized by an irresistible urge to write, like never before, if there hadn't been any paper there I would have had to write on the blanket, last week, five o'clock in the afternoon I had an epiphany in a waking state while I was writing, that was perhaps an indication I should penetrate into the difficulties. . .

I stammered foot prayers, washed my teeth with an almond,

delivery now by the basket twice a week! The many books, never, as long as I live, will I be able to finish reading them all, but I wish for it with all my heart! (The wickerwork of the basket-cover aired until something from its depths: a rising pair of wings? and with outstretched wings seemed to hover toward the top and there to disappear into the open air. . .), oh what spiral notes, tufts of hair between my fingers, our lifetime soon consumed. Recently rediscovered a picture of me in my youth, I call, then I understood that *there must have been a different me at one time*, can you follow me? That's not just by chance, calls JULIAN, while I show him the pictures in the family album for the nth time, your grandmother a beauty, your mother, each of them must have been a beauty, your father! the red figures, flaming figures on the outermost edge, beautiful masks with flaming mouths, calls JULIAN, the beautiful masks from whose mouths the flaming tongues shoot forth, an outermost edge of the bed.

At five o'clock in the morning, I say, the decline of words thus decline of the moon, fire ball, skull place of the sun, while it pulled up its purple skull dripping out of the white-gray cloud masses, slowly let it appear, I saw in the double mirror of the eye glasses that I had taken down and held in my hands for a moment the small glowing point and behind it the window cross. The angel of the glasses which is able to hold liquids so that one can bring them to one's mouth, effortlessly, and can swallow them without having to slurp from a bottle, pitcher, or container, the angel touches my lips: what an invention! to concede a temporary solidity to liquid substances, oh how happy we can be. The loose bolts of the honeysuckle over the fences, violin and iris, weeping cypress, the dun straw in the barrels, ready to be burned, and the new yellow-green blossoms on the house fronts, parrot-blossoms, now late in the year, I call, it looks like the return of spring, the warm drops on the window-panes, upon emotional stimulation I try to endure this parrot language, while the young yellow-green blossoms, tropical parrot blossoms burst forth again everywhere. . .

on stork legs, black headscarf of a Turkish widow, an emerging truth, I call to JULIAN, do you remember, immediately after his death my mother and Polly tried to talk each other into believing that the dead person had taken this or that for himself as a sign that he was still among us, they wanted to convince me of it too, but I wasn't sure. Then however the ostensibly missing objects that had perhaps followed him for only part of the way suddenly reappeared. . .

after the departure of a landscape, so that certain daily tasks are always accompanied by the same memory images, when for example I cast the first glance in the mirror in the morning, recent memories of walks in Paris appear, also the view of the small electrical shop across from the institute where we stayed whose display windows were glaringly pierced by the afternoon sun when I, heading for the nearby post office, went past them at that time of day. . .

in the morning then the changed relations in my head namely in the resonance chamber it sounded different from before, I tap my skull with a tuning fork, where is the flesh of my head, my bones hurt, teeth are lost in dream. I cry about everything, the bold mountains fall on the beautiful sun, the shadow swans at my place, many staircases in my head that are used by thousands of people, the open weather, I call, that causes me pain, it meshes so, I call, in my head, all the concealed truths, are waiting for me to invent them, rescue them or how should I say, the massive scale of my eyes focussed on the instruments of my doctor, I call, I lie there, almost lose consciousness, possibly he exerts a hypnotic effect, sprinkled with vinegar, I ask him, did you sprinkle my head with vinegar, all life notes are within reach, also the silver spoon in the west, odor of musk on the edge of the hand, I have become electrical, attract electrical impulses, dizzying pasture leaves in front of my eyes, whose shadows moved by the wind are shivering across the path, the sparks are visibly emitted from my finger tips, from the balls of my hands, now the work will also be increasingly difficult, an ever-greater haste accompanies ever-sharper observations, my experience of the world is comparable to falling into a funnel, *who among us has looked into the heart of a father. . .*

his extremely thin smile, the alert squinting eyes turned toward the light, his back to the darkness. . . why do the same memory sequences continually recur, I call, as soon as I think about him, as soon as I have to think about the deceased person, why have so very few particulars remained in my mind? How he runs the fingers of his right hand through the side of his hair, thereby looking at himself in the mirror in the front hall, moves to a profile position in the mirror; how he, returning home, tosses his gray-green hat with a lively swing and brings it safely to a landing on top of the coat rack, how he, slipping out of his shoes, sinks into his rocking chair, how he then sits quietly in his rocker and looks straight ahead, arms and hands pressed to the side rests, entwined with them, how his narrow mouth smiles thoughtfully. Did he sense something of his role, of his unchanging greatness, of his balancing effect? sometimes he got directly into my speech, I mean by way of looking he got into my language, oh, I call, soon the outlines begin to grow weaker. . . on a light ford or foot, raven that scoops water, the eyes so lovingly around his head, his skull lighted from behind, bears a slender halo, there is an intertwined memory or like multiple exposures of a photographic film, the date pit in the middle of the room, I call, scent mark and an echoing bark, scene of the flesh. . . there are no witnesses, I say, but it's true I mean I perhaps dreamt it like everything else, with LERCH and the others, all of that is however only conjecture, or my notes only imagine things, an organ tone when I breathe, we often exchanged bones, stations like flugelhorns in this never-ending night. . . also gloomily excited by LERCH'S letters in which he made analytic observations, then blurred them again lovingly, I sat leaning over his table or sofa, the whole night, but how far I was driven by desire I don't know, sky- and sea-murmuring sofa. . . the earrings that I liked to wear best I could no longer take off. . . *and the twinkling towns like small buttons.* . .

to have become the self-conscious timorous aging child, I call, from whose hands objects fall, who clumsily stumbles over any obstacle, turns around in annoyance, and tries to get out of the way of any difficulty, can understandably be neither interesting nor attractive for others but rather repulsive and ridiculous, thus I was beyond help, regardless of place, regardless of situation, neither do I find the right way of behaving anymore, set myself up only in my hideout, where my typing fingers fly over the keys, in happy frenzy. . .

the truth is, calls JULIAN, our disappointments in life and the world are mercifully offset by our ability to write, without this writing ability we would have gone mad long ago, in all points of view it depends on *whether one is shaken into position, after sleeping, and each time in excitement, or fever frost*. . . I'll write that out IN GREEN while still lying in bed in the morning, I call, with a bright green felt pen, the cap of which resembles a snow-white wool cap pulled far down over one's face, *"must get Goya more het-up"*. . . was written on a note, I found it under my pillow, also heavenly image then I was often giddy precisely there, I mean on the even stretch. Torturing (Trieste), washable parquet floor. . . thus moss-green walls, exposed to the DOG COMPLEX like every morning: something smells or tastes like that, or at night when I try to suppress attacks of difficulty in breathing (panting). . . they, big as well as small, always look at me on the street as if I were in fact one of them, would like to draw me more closely into their world, sometime, deal with their way of thought, occupy myself with their world of feeling, there could be remarkable parallels to my own structure also standpoint, I say, they would presumably assimilate me immediately, I say, then I would be totally monopolized, in any case for some time. . . I recognize myself again then with flier's hat shower cap in the mirror, melancholy heraldic animal, new moon. . . my watch-glass window has awakened. . . a shadow on the street, the shadow stops then in front of the lighted store window as if it wanted to observe something as if it wanted to inspect something, I remember the evening *when I went past the shadow of my mother,* I wanted to call to the driver, stop! stop! but the word got stuck in my throat, she went past as a shadow, she stopped in front of the store window, looked at it a long time, but it seemed to me, she only whisked by then, she whisked by like a specter and I wasn't sure whether it was she although winter coat fur collar umbrella, that would all have been right. . .

No one. Nothing. But I saw someone on the street in nice clothes, the store windows shone, effusive pneumatic dispatch. Thus green walls, in memory *such a green rain,* I call, every perceptual experience seems to indicate to me experiences of ENTRANCE and APPEARANCE, I remember for example an initial meeting decades ago with the German scholar and author R.E. and his lady friend at our summer place, Espang Allerheiligen, it was raining heavily, we had picked them up at the train station, I have the image this RAIN IMAGE deep inside me—I don't know anymore what we talked about, only that a pleased pleasing aura surrounded the two of them, then we drove together up the mountain, they stayed with us a few days, once we went mushroom hunting and it turned out that he was a passionate and knowledgeable mushroom collector, last September, before we were to meet him again after so many years, we had no idea anymore what he looked like, we didn't know how we were supposed to recognize him in the midst of the party guests, I recognized him again however immediately, contrary to my assumption that he should look like my friend F.W.—

Their mutual ENTRANCE and APPEARANCE however seemed definitely past and gone, they disappeared in fact suddenly as if in a forest, in a green scene also rain scene dabbed with white and pink dogroses, I still hear but only from a distance tempest trumpet whirlwind, oh I've split a rib. . .

the angry hissing and rumbling, and while the wind plays the jew's-harp in the garden, thus the BANDAGE. And how everything hurls around in my head, I mean that with the mushrooms, it continually drags behind in me like a tow, my eyes flow over from it, the stones flow over in white and pink, the hills, the valleys, damp-warm weather, winter spring. The raven that scooped water comes close to my bed, I'm not surprised that the water for example doesn't dry up in the kitchen, in the bathroom, even the objects in the drawer feel damp to the touch, did it rain in, drip down? now also on the house front across the way the WATCH-GLASS WINDOW, on one of the upper windows, moved to a daytime scene I lie in the damp hollow of my eyes. The tears collect there, I feel how the water dams up; when I hear music immediately upon waking with a completely blank consciousness, I can also see them, suddenly, startled, saw Mozart a few days ago! namely first became aware of his musical figure with eyes closed, a casual concept from the beginning, I say, the organ of laughter at the root of the heart . . . the watery blue in the sockets in the eye sockets, from the whole heaven and earth, a furious copulation namely with words, very similar courses, completely similar courses, thus moved moving LOVE WORK. The lower part is an arm, a wing, a green rain in memory. . . sometimes falteringly then again everything by leaps and bounds. . . my remembrances, my memories. . . . in the morning I couldn't remember to whom I had written the day before THAT I WOULD BE LOOKING FORWARD TO HIS VISIT IN FEBRUARY, which in general is totally untrue, I call, I hardly ever look forward to a visit from anyone anymore, from any point of view, and to tell the truth, every sentence should be a message, I'm imagining all of that, pneumatic dispatch system, in the despicable dress (low-down), *looking deeply into the citrus fruit,* speech and gesture of embarrassment, hurts my left eye, defenseless I race away, cutting axils on the buds of plants still tightly closed or "my eyes always look to the Lord," archaic occulist, work on the left eye, etc.

You called you came into the room, the decline of words, the decline of the sun on July 18th, we exchange emotive words *(in the human light,* or *sheet lightning, completely oceanic, "immortal poppy").* On that night side you cut me off so that I hear voices, furthermore can also see the NATURAL IMAGE of your figure, bordered by green. When I look at red. A month ago, on the day before my birthday I woke up with a letter to you, I call, had trouble writing it down however as usual, one likes to blur the difference: bygone for example going. By the way, I saw you, if it was not a double, in Budapest not far from Keleti on August 31st, but I didn't approach you because I had the impression you might feel you were being followed, was it in fact you or did I project you onto the person who passed in front of me and suddenly turned into a clothing arcade on the right, such things do occur. . .

and no purpose: this my life without any purpose, no purpose whatsoever, or how should I say it. Almost covered over by the murmuring of the sea, later illusory, I saw it myself: with closed eyes, his head alternately raised and lowered to the book in his hand, a young man memorizing, on the train platform next to me. . . the stenographic symbol of hair, in the wash basin: BUT STILL. (But still?). . .

Noises of the motor of a parking car, the ear substitutes for the eye, sounds like polyphonic obsessional chirping of birds, or smacking *kisses* fresh from the kitchen, those harmless blown-off kisses for children, placed noisily and with puckered lips, so that anyone can hear it, the date pit in the middle of the room,

or an emitting, hurling out ("hurling out and everything!"),
coughing out, unpleasant rattling in the throat, something from
which one wants to distance oneself, detach and free oneself:
despicable SCUM. -
Life. Nothing. It becomes somewhat more difficult. Long
reflection, sudden recoil, it doesn't mean anything
(musk/labiatae). Nothing. Long pause. Still nothing. God is in
my heart (half a heart form), the hook below, the support in
God, he flies over walls and mountains, the lower part is an
arm, a wing. . .
And there are also the windmill wings that already lay me
contorted at your feet again, I say, this entire insane entangle-
ment, I say, Spanish is proud thus let me lie there. It is the
dusk (the demon), the CUTTING OFF. That I would like to go
out with an eye shield, crash helmet, face mask, visor, and
persevering, I say to my mother (as a child), or he, LERCH,
says to his mother—but, how does he actually address
her?—then he cowers (as a child, to his dog) and watches how
the steam rises from it, I say, and then he squats down to the
animal and watches, how the steaming excrement slowly sinks
to the ground, but the leash was already caught in it, namely the
rope. The head tilted to the side thus turned, in order to be able
to see everything carefully. . .
just like a trafficator (signal) borrowed from the motorized
nineteen-thirties, I call, it was fun to watch at that time, red
signal flag, stretched-out red-gloved finger, patrol cop in red,
could be folded out in the direction in which one wanted to go,
extremely simple to use, application of a simple push-button
system, the application of a trivial fantasy indeed seems to have
become anachronistic like the narrative stance itself so that the
friendly comment YOU HAVE SHOWN IMAGINATION sounds
rather derogatory. "Moon of the long snow," on the telephone. . . I am a Red Hawk Indian. . . perhaps the IN-
BETWEEN TALE still legitimate, I don't know, I call, perhaps
yet the course of the IN-BETWEEN TALE, like under hypnosis,
at breakfast the GLACIER BUTTER for example, now at nine
in the morning my room is strewn with thyme, and camomile,
mint, when I return in three or four days the aroma will still be
there, the bundles of herbs are lying on my small oval table
(Orly table, as Polly admiringly observed), on the night side I'm

a Red Hawk Indian, am cuckoo-speckled, a giant fluffed-up
partridge, also monster, dreamt again about giant cuckoo birds,
acoustic key image? bewitching eye scan?
And of course I include my daily reading material, the red
signal flag. Also you and LERCH and Polly, what do I know,
that is the whole world: involuntary SIGNAL GIVERS, I say,
whereas I myself cannot act as a SIGNAL GIVER, cannot be
helpful to anyone as a SIGNAL GIVER, in any case I can't
imagine it. This neighborhood, this continual cracking of bones
next door, or when they break apart the small chopped-up
things, I don't know. Thus the purest distraction, diversion,
temptation, constantly at the mercy of the clumsy rattling noise
next door!, I call, now winter is already here. Heavenly child
it's almost in vain that I am in the world, I like best to go
barefoot, my hands and feet, receiver and transmitter! Transmitter for no one. Can you tell me why I must stare continually
at that WATCH-GLASS WINDOW, in the tower room across
the way, the storm shook me up, that meshes so, sun in my
head, in the storm wind yesterday I saw the street sweep down:
female figurehead, with uneven, no, braided black hair on her
back, the glowing butt boldly in front between her lips, threw
it away then still glowing, thus against the wind, against the
stream, the untimely attracts me, suits me or how should I say
it, I mean it became clear to me in a particular way, also
everything else you talk about. Like in a dream, I say, when one
can't seem to get away although one moves forward at a high
speed, in entirely *unhampered* language, right after that everything formulated very carefully and precisely again, changes in
tempo, like soul-birds (sirens), most rigid in the *human light!*
and how this frail, this grandiose life is always still *prolonged*
a bit! But still! (But still?)
And I say to my mother (as a child), or he says to his
mother (as a child), I'm talking about LERCH, then he reaches
over the table and stretches out his hand to her and she immediately starts to plow and comb on his underarm, the inside of his
wrist, such gentle scratching, I say, actually the dream is
gone. . .
how to live, how to live here, unfastening the arms the legs,
how to live here and stand up to the world. . . on a light
stream, the stalking, the beautiful seeing, this *prolonging* pro-

longed life from year to year. And always lived a life of caution, and of cowering, memorizing, repeating and giving in, what do I know, this my dog-like character. This my degenerate state of mind, everything only appearance, only for appearance, apparent adaptation, and apparent submission, that doesn't make the people I know more favorably disposed to me, my readership, testators, doctors, publishers for example, or what should I call it.

To tell the truth, I call, my head isn't with it, I taste the change of perceptions, recognize their natural progression, see everything as possibly superimposed on everything else, TO BE ON THE ROAD THROUGH THE EXPRESS MESSENGER, and similar crash landings in seconds, inexplicable world transformations also, the intertwined mountains in their length and breadth. . .

and during the trip, the contours of the mountains, I say, seemed to imitate one another in various layers and shadings of gray-violet, each hilltop imitated the one above it, as it were, and so forth continually, in five or six rising levels, similarly the hollows replicated themselves down to the flatter dips, so that one involuntarily had to think of an intertwined canon of tones whose echo seemed to adjust itself to the movements of one's own body, also to mark the movements of consciousness in gentle ecstasy, so that I wanted to ask myself, *is it paradisal?*— These fields of mullein (flannel-leaf) flooded by the late afternoon September light, a thousand-fold candle light spun over the meadows, the graves, flickering moor landscapes, fantasized tableaux, we get off later the lights in back while the wind plays the jew's-harp in the garden, thus the BANDAGE. . . (then I lowered the image half way, namely the lid, or like Moses over the sea of reeds. . .)

oh the lightning-loaded nerve-loaded things. . . had almost lost my senses, from there the SENTIMENTAL WALTZ that my grandfather played on his small accordion, and I as a little TYKE astride his knee. . . the red summer, the old land house swarmed by bees, titanic bats for example, desert fox, Egyptian red point, the sun also purple when I close my eyes, from any point of view: plumage? butterfly? a color that is not particularly becoming to me, flips all too easily over into green, and highly smudged the bluish pink of the arteries (Andes?), carmine red bodies wherever I look, also bordered by green, thus shadows dipped in paint, intertwined shimmering asphalt images at night, reflecting, in the rain, corn roses, damp garlands, iris, poppy, minstrel of tender calligraphy. . . long apple, pomegranate, then that small dog howled like a screech owl, I could hardly sleep, perceived something like TWIN SMELLS in the stairway this morning, alternating between acetone and bananas, the smells seemed however to blend for a few seconds, then to separate again immediately, the banana smell went with the color blue, the acetone with yellow in contrast. . . the racers straight away, not to be detained, in my head, I call, blowing on it, in my head. . . *the next book, I say, will be a very smooth book, but this one, this one here can still be a bit outside the norm, thus unkempt, toward the rakish—wild,* and always so roving, my tale of woe dog-like. On the back of the dog there was snow, this outburst of laughter in dogs' faces for example, no one can recognize it, but they laugh! the organ of laughter at the root of the heart, the bafflement, the wishes, the gaze, unique, the dexterity besides the heaviness and sluggishness of large dogs, everything in one moment, when I for example in the early morning, or upon coming home at night am *disoriented* in some way or another, then all sorts of terrible things happen to me, I call, from exhaustion I mean I cause bad things to happen, bump into things, cut and scratch myself until wounded, get caught in appliances and objects lying around, stumble and fall, *while tearing at my hair,* I make dumb mistakes then, things get into my eye. . . or a type of flying. . .

("undressed and uncoated. . ." . . . preferably the naked truth. . .), unfastening the arms the legs, how to live, how to live here and stand up to the world? am known as a coward also cowardess, what do I know, a hybrid form, who is it that always sewed my mouth shut? later the lilac is reflected in the window, the early May day takes me under its blue wings, eyes and ears dive down in the light roof of leaves, am still sober, haven't yet spoken a word to anyone, an extensive illness based on sensory deception, I call, presumably a pollen disease, or seminal emission an uninterrupted emission in my brain, and while he, LERCH, hurries past me through the hall, past me and touches me gently with a sideways glance. . . YOU'VE PUT ON

MAKE-UP. . . MADE-UP FOR A CHANGE... a shudder in me, a long feeling of arousal, flowers on the edge of the flesh, as if he had touched me with consecrated box-tree branches, a cautious sitting-up, foaming, running-over, flowing-away. . . this colossus, I call, mammoth bones, these wonderful mammoth bones which like pillars are ready to carry my body around at any time while my true head somewhere in the trees—

feel myself ageless, maybe seven years old, in my gym shoes, long dress, *with messenger bag* and in general singing, freshly sewed and hemmed, I stood in the meadow, the playing children however ran in. Whatever my feet could carry, whatever my eyes could hold, I write otherwise in the sky, my ears in the shutter, *like a shepherd's child because my throat is so thin*, washed my teeth with an almond, lashed my ear lobes with a fresh stinging nettle, actually beat, I call, I hear it slapping, the stinging nettle slaps against his ear, LERCH'S ear, I see that his ear soon becomes dark red, entries on the flying intention, or seen together like NIGHTINGALE AND NEEDLE, perceiving the world so lively and fine with such rested nerves in the morning, I say, that everything seems connected to everything else, everything suggests an association with everything else, every network of thoughts immediately wants to be spun out further, and other high-flying landscapes. The flying eye for example, held against the light against the day, the bold mountains fell on the beautiful sun and the blooming hills covered us up. . .

I remember, I call, when he entered my room for the first time, he didn't ask, as most visitors do, WHETHER I COULD STILL FIND ANYTHING HERE, rather he said only YOU CAN'T GET OUT OF HERE, and perhaps he meant that I had gotten into a trap, whereby he wasn't wrong, although sometimes I succeed in opening one of the two windows, I explained: then I can step out, look from the garden over the tree-lined street and toward the west at the outlines of the mountains that surround our city; also at night, when I get up, when I in my constant restlessness can't sleep any more, I feel very happy, when the stars appear to me in the glowing window-cut and the moon in its aura or darkened by yellow-gray cloud veils: and sails away then precisely over my zenith, a decline of the moon, a decline of words, I write then in the

sky, the pretty stationery with the parrot seal, the letter place
rustles like silk, a renewal a digression a pink doll's arm on the
parquet floor, indications of a hypnotic future where everything
seems to be driven out onto the smallest possible contact
area. . .
The book comes again aqueousness, these changes in me
what should I call it. . . upon emotional stimulation I try to
endure this parrot language, the story doesn't exist anymore,
maybe an account of a specific condition, something that takes
place not only within a matter of days, weeks, and months, but
also intensifies at particular points to a spark-emitting spherical
ball, I cry and cry (for joy), or how should I say it. The warmth
of the morning, last time *(death time)* we sat in groups in a
roomy apartment, we moved close together on the side opposite
the doors, suddenly one of the white door panels opened and I
saw that it concealed a television set, it flickered and sounded
forth, and the hostess shifted the door panel a bit so I could see
the screen better, then however one of the other people shifted
the door to a different angle so that he could see better, and it
went on like that, someone was always adjusting the door panel,
a terrible weariness of life came over me suddenly with such
force that tears came to my eyes, then I could view the people
only with repulsion, those who had previously been so near to
me, I was suddenly so disgusted with every one of them that I
couldn't stand to be together with them in a room, I got up,
took one last look at the groups of friends who were apparently
surprised and went out, but a loud laugh from all sides accompanied my exit, actually the dream is gone, I call, meridians
that flow through my body, thus dumbfounded, I call, trace of
fresh blood, I followed the trace of blood on my nocturnal walk
through the streets, hoping I wouldn't fall down after that small
incident, the NEVERTHELESS of the seas (fairies) is always
very important, the head knows every step, the windswept
bushes on the edge of the street, these changes in me, what
should I attribute them to, wild birds flew from red trees, field
delphinium bloomed dark violet. With plumage. With grasshoppers on my feet. . . there is constancy also comfort in nature,
I call, in the course of the seasons, today there's a strong wind,
the sky whitish-blue, from the climbing plants that go up the
stone wall, sometimes bunches of seeds sweep past my window

to the top of one of the monkey-bread trees breaking apart with luxuriant growth, a tiny spider has spun her net there, snowed with cherry blossoms. Musk and rose-poppy, mixture of stars. Those wild and ecstatic gestures of nature, I call, with which it gets through to us again and again, dagger point of a spring, I call, so that a wounded melancholy remains in my heart, this merciful rain-drop feeling, caressing cheek and forehead, also baptismal bath, tender mania, extensive steppe grass. . .

my thoughts coil their knots more tightly around me, orchid or its equal, his farewell kiss made a black mark on my cheek, I'm talking about LERCH, a fire truck whisked by, we try to figure out how long we've known each other, it amounts to twenty, thirty and more weeks, months, years. . .

A phenomenon, calls JULIAN, that one doesn't like to see when someone you know abandons himself without opposition to the process of aging, also admits to it. A phenomenon we wish for, that out of consideration for us he would maintain the pose of being unspent, the appearance of indestructibility through time. A phenomenon of our desire, that he would spare us that for a long time, that he for a long time would not call us to be witnesses of that humiliating inevitability and outrageous despicableness of constant aging, *"sighing and crying" (Goya).*

Orchid or its equal. . . I wear white feet (gulls) at present, secret surf, at the bottom of my creativity now, to protest, I call, or how should I say it. Over the crest of the hill, nourished only by nettles, having become entirely green I flew over the crest of the mountains, got lost in the forest and wandered around for three hours, then came a heavy hail storm, it rose over the neighboring wine gardens, as a death laundry. . . have become very vulnerable, didn't notice anything of my injury at first, feelings of deep discomfort gradually, this outbreak of tears (nerve storm). The worst is of course how the outside world pushes to the fore and intrudes and harasses and worries and drives us into a corner with its possessive demands, day and night, so that we finally feel forced to withdraw completely, to become a HOMO CLAUSUS—if we were not however at the last minute called back to something like our *natural condition,* or what should I call it. For since we feel increasingly less able to relate to our surroundings, indeed since it is hardly possible anymore to maintain even the most superficial contacts, we

experience suddenly from one minute to the next something like
a REVERSAL: suddenly from one minute to the next we thus
experience ourselves as our own INVERSE IMAGE; we suddenly want to attach ourselves to anyone, want a sense of
community with everyone, involve ourselves, equalize, want to
lean on, snuggle up to, smuggle in everywhere—oh mutual eye
and ear, brain, headdress, antlers, foot, hand, and mouth. . . a
before and after, feel almost numb, the indentation from last
night in my cheek, on the my cheek and side of my head as I
read propped up, the last pages of the book, advice and glossary,
captivating commentary, the pockmark on my left cheek,
dropsical, suddenly faded in the mirror upon more careful
scrutiny / slid on foot over large areas of water. . . waking
experiences mix now increasingly unhindered with those of
dream, I call, this morning a sudden darkness that comes over
the entire visible sky, I saw it myself, the snow blew steadily in
tiny flakes, I don't draw the drapes at night anymore now, thus
I see the stars and the moon, they flicker above the gable across
the way, a letter from LERCH, Indian, Chinese, inbetween
Mongolian, I don't know, written in violet ink, today Andreas
fourth, February, Friday, found myself in a gloomy mood, was
awakened early by pink-tinged snow light, I call, a snow plow
races down the street, shoots through the street, flies hurriedly
past below my window. . .
    with lowered head in the flower room, sweat emerged silver
from the double bass player, I saw it myself, the woman a treble
clef, something iridescent between major and minor keys, the
story doesn't exist anymore, equipment of a twitching sun snake
or something like that. Having a narrative form? But what narrative form can be relied upon, what narrative form is still
defensible, we don't want to have a story told to us anymore,
we don't want to have to tell a story anymore, the strife-torn
feelings, the gestures that have set in resort to repetitive
mechanisms, hypnotic cycle, a principle of repetition culled from
life. . . thus polysemantically aroused, an excitement of the
senses, the heart, or what should I call it.
    Furious yarrow, it was lightning outside—it's a long time
ago I was a child and it snowed. . .
    The tongue pastries in the middle of a dream, and there
were two lines from a poem by Poe to be read at the lower

edge, as if from a blackboard at school. But I didn't remember them upon awakening, shortly before that one of the Three Kings, the handsome Moor, trudged with flat feet over a snow path, the two plastic sacks that he carried like weights seemed to pull down his arms, threatened to stretch them out to great lengths. . . fur cap instead of diadem. . . the white bones of the mouth. . . the fine shimmering snakes of the head. . . to do everything preferably with only one hand, the other hand watching *idly,* because one is always distracted, no, because one's attention is focused on the continuation of a course, solely in the second itself.

At that time, with LERCH, I call, ran down the steep garden path, to the frozen pond, the swaying bluetits in the branches made crackling noises. The zebra, questioned LERCH while running, what was it actually with the zebra, was it its markings, its look—or what did you find so engaging? It was an important experience for me, I said, the animal stood there, didn't move, looked deep into my eyes. Later it chased around a bit in its enclosure, but it seemed to me as if it occurred in a *dream of the animal,* it chased around a bit, but so unreal, so on the borders of its consciousness that I had to cry. It seemed to want to reveal some sort of secret, a message that didn't reach me, I mean there wasn't much of a gap, but then in the last minute I couldn't understand it after all. . . that message, which I apparently lacked the prerequisites for deciphering, occupied me a long time, did not let me rest for a long time. . . now my hair stands on end, my brain cells sometimes take on the form of dolphins, my abilities clearly slacken, in a strong and angry expression of pain I scream everything into myself without uttering even the slightest sound, a muddled role distribution, thus I scream everything into myself, without anyone knowing about it, and hoofing it down the mountain, all of that is however only conjecture, coloratura, cadence, I call, upon emotional stimulation I try to endure this parrot language, in his letter to the Corinthians Paul said SPEAKING IN TONGUES IS NOT A RATIONAL WAY OF SPEAKING, and he was taken to be mad, etcetera.

These changes in me, what should I attribute them to, noises of the water, reed fingers on my lips, sinewy throat. . . the bearded woman at the crossroads. . . AIR GAL. . . now and

then a woman with a beard like a burial woman from the underworld, led me somewhere toward home, I say, like a Christ
figure she lay in the middle of the bed, her crying children right
and left, a boy and a girl, the one child *like a nut like James in
ecstasy,* later I saw how the two children leaned against the
unkempt overgrown bushes bordering the road, rigid brushwork
that easily bore the weight of the children, then I saw how they
pushed and shoved each other into that thorny thicket and how
they seemed to sink into it screaming, while blood sprang forth
on their arms and legs. . . *here is a different style,* says JULIAN,
extensive passages namely as melancholic woman. . .

I made an analysis at twenty-five and at forty-five, the pain
in my stomach and kidneys contributed its share, I tried everything possible, began the analysis again. . . for seven months,
seven years, no seventeen years I took the opportunity but it
proved to be wrong. . .

The burial woman possessed female and male gender characteristics, leaned over me while I slept, *actually the dream is
gone,* she was a czar (czarina), can be a pearl in my life, or a
team of birds, is it the glow of both genders?

I live depressed and exhausted and do the wrong thing, have
spread myself too thinly over the people and things around me,
but that's not right either, I want to get lost. I've become highly
electrical, I electrify myself everywhere, the sparks fly visibly
from my fingertips. I also miss the train, time gets away from
me, I don't have any time anymore, it seems to me that I've
never had so little time as in these years, the truth is, I have
increasingly less time at my disposal, I am too late in my time.

The phone booth embushed by green, the mountains to be
feared, the field of vision completely rolled out, with all eyes
and ears, forehead eye (overbra), or it's like when someone says
THE BODY ITSELF KNOWS BEST, I want to survive as
quickly as possible, without pain, a neurotic relation to my sense
organs, or what should I call it, otitis for more than five weeks,
I call, and can hardly expect recovery, but maybe *in the name
of my father.* . .

It's the stalking, the beautiful seeing, the secret safeguard,
the digging in luxury, thus notice, message and announcement,
that's the free hunting ground in which I move, or whatever, but
no one notices anything of this performance, I saw it myself, the

amputated arms of the tree on the side of the street, I felt it myself, the cut areas were cemented gray-brown to prevent sprouting. . . quickly quickly before I start to cry, hydrant as zebra, drunk boy drags empty bottle behind him, I remember that girl that beauty, with a zebra hairdo, I saw it myself, I saw a woman with a zebra hairdo, she had dyed black-white horizontal stripes in her hair, a most unlikely decor, I call, there are no witnesses but it's true, I mean I often dreamt it, *and it's already gone again*. . .

a yellow airship above the roofs, we eat small dragons the moon, my pipe-father and I, the tightening in my throat as soon as I see him in front of me, in my memory, I see him also as a yellow ship above the clouds, all in good time, I expect everything from him, I say, can you follow me, I expect everything from it, namely from this Sunday mass held in his behalf, *in the name of my father,* and the fact that I suffered from this illness for weeks, indeed months and still suffer, I can attribute finally only to my indecision about having a holy mass held. I meet the sexton, he is sitting behind a desk and slips on a chasuble while still sitting, I step back startled but he tells me to come closer. For whom, he asks, for whom should this mass be held, every sentence a statement, every sentence a message, I hold back with my idea of intercession for my own well-being, explain instead that it's for my father, in commemoration of my father, I say, Franz Xaver, I say, as intention. Will it be received? He makes out a receipt, how much, he asks then, day and hour, as donation. . . the many trumpets, I say, before leaving, thus trombones, and someone also beat the drums, but the similarity to a cherub, I call, I immediately noticed the similarity to a cherub of one of the musicians, apparently the youngest one, the drop trace for example, fresh blood, the jet-black eyes on the pale background, sweat emerged momentarily from the double bass player, I saw it myself, a silvery green remained as trace, a nonidentifiable bang from the street startled me, the yellow ship, lonely cloud ship has entered the area.

I can't talk while going upstairs, one shouldn't talk while walking, etcetera, a mental apparition, here as well as there, also I'm always looking for something without knowing what it is, warm and soft like a breast, when I for example climb the stairs to my place with the mail that has just arrived, I get too little air, climbing the stairs gives me trouble, I toss the mail on the bed, on the table, on the empty chairs, here as well as there, piece by piece opened with joyful haste, scanned, read, here as well as there in search of something, I don't know what, some kind of promise, news, a coded message, what should I call it, am in search of something, but I don't know what, when for example I open a book, lay it aside again soon after that because I couldn't find what I was looking for, or because my desire to find something although I don't know what it is was not satisfied, we stand under a current, but the switch remains off, and so forth. I lay the book aside, perhaps I'll pick it up again later, I often find books in my apartment that contain old bookmarks from my earliest youth for example like lifemarks. Lately there have in general been only two or three books that I could read to the end, they satisfied me completely in that they aroused as well as allayed my curiosity, the truth is, I took notes from them almost continually, it intrigued and satisfied me in a pleasing way, and there was never a moment when I had to ask myself if and why I should read further. . . stationery store gray and white, when the sunlight suddenly penetrates, dive and fly, the lilac is reflected in the window, the early day takes me under its wing, eyes and ears dive down in the light roof of leaves, dislocation of the senses, gleaming at five in the morning, snowed with cherry blossoms, white roses, every sentence should be a message, with constant correction of course, crossed-out passages for example, rapport, the sober dates, precise inventory, I fall on my knees and begin to pray, the friction between the soul and the outside world, I trudge through the plains, through the woods, and in general I often don't know what day it is, I sit up in the semi-darkness, now the night is almost over, the journey completed.

This my writing, I call, pursues me even in my dreams, keeps me awake for hours, wakes me up early in the morning, after interrupted sleep, *but one cannot expect acclaim for this kind of prayer fantasies. . . :* by chance someone said the word in my presence so that I was startled. . . upon emotional stimulation I try to endure this parrot language, while the young yellow-green blossoms, tropical parrot blossoms burst forth again everywhere. . . like a shepherd's child, or at that time with LERCH, I say, because my throat is too thin, etcetera, the moon is actually capable of waning, finally he felt himself all too burdened by me, because I increasingly came to recognize his competence and also let him know it I mean I couldn't and didn't want to withdraw from the all too obvious certainty of his existence, my dependence on him increased in equal measure, and my dependence remained for years thereafter, I say, on his fleetingness, flight (common courtesy) and so forth, like with you and me in the first years, but it was also almost like a trump, thus I played my last card, or what should I say, was always, since childhood, have always been in search of something, I could never imagine what it could be, first you, then LERCH. Or the other way around, what do I know, the borders are fluid, the outlines dissolve, I often don't know anymore where it begins and ends with you or LERCH, can you follow me, but sometimes of course one thinks one has done everything wrong, doesn't want to know anything more at all about those years of life, is almost ashamed of such a past, that is presumably the reason one doesn't want to bring up one's past, that is also the reason one refuses to let others bring it up, that is probably also the reason one hasn't preserved any memories, or as good as none. And actually one is ready to deny one's own past completely, I say, this life of failure. And in a kind of panic one sees the time that remains shrink together into nothing, everything too short, I call, everything measured too narrowly to allow a person to begin all over again. . .

everything done wrong, it's all only lies, a sham, none of it is true, or I only invented it, but I want to retract it, everything too short, I say, everything measured too narrowly, this our period of time, what do I know, I'm on the night side, am a Red Hawk Indian, and cuckoo-speckled, there's a sea that rocks from one side of my forehead to the other, continually back and forth so that I become very dizzy, bewitching EYE SCAN, storm trip and water crash: THE DERANGEMENT OF AN EMBRACE, or acoustic after-images, as you call it, my thoughts have allegedly gone mad because of that. . . sound and din, when it cracks next door in the early morning, remorse, despondency, it sounds like bones cracking, *I wear white feet (gulls) at present,* I have been in Espang Allerheiligen the whole night now, I call, or Himalaya, sounds of the beating of water, and the cracking of bones, the rocks rang endlessly, they are collecting in the skies now, I call, they move to the sleep trees in the western part of the city, rehearse it anew each day, they rehearse the final break-away, when no one is watching, almost no one watches, the streams of attachment flow under the most disparate things, then I write in the air, I mean I write in my notebook without looking, I sit up in the semi-darkness, one shouldn't talk while walking, I can't talk while going upstairs, it prevents the insights, disturbs the connections, I've always had a special liking for reticent people, with LERCH however it was different, he was always the closest one to me, at the same time the most incomprehensible and the most distant, I often took refuge in silence when I didn't know how to go on for example, the reticence helped me and was good for me each time, JULIAN and I often sit together for hours in silence, with LERCH however it was always different, we talked for nights, went from one thing to another, couldn't stop, precious hours. . . sometimes I literally tried to force a meeting with him, I mean I almost compelled him, and I benefited from it: I gained advantage from it for my *writing,* since a meeting with him elicited a sustained pleasant arousal of my entire mental and physical being, I could, so to speak, count on that condition to set in, I could depend on the fact that from such effects an advantage would emerge for my *writing:* to the extent that I felt exposed to his powerful influence, it afterwards sent me back all the more intensely to my isolated self, which, even if eclipsed by the temporary separation, felt itself abundantly enriched and stimulated. So that at times, when my work threatened to come to a standstill, I *intentionally tried to stage* such a meeting with him.

Thus we ran a long time, always in a circle around the frozen garden pond, which seemed to be speckled with fallen decaying leaves, we ran with large flying steps, in the icy February air, then the talking stopped, we were no longer talkative: our breath was visible in front of our lips, in the overheated restaurant in which we finally took refuge, a pale streak of lightning in the white water in the white glass, the fire trucks raced howlingly past, I poured and poured from the bottle although the glass threatened to run over, had long since run over, I did it with my physical being with my entire physical being. . .

in the interest of truth, I saw it myself, I saw the flashes of lightning before my eyes again, an injury the doctor said, serious affront (attack), thus the years raced by, where will we land (end)? The fears overwhelm me, the language of the other side is hard to learn, I must however gradually learn to overcome the fear of death, you are conspicuous, says my PROMPTER, but of inconspicuous character, like a shepherd's child because the throat is so thin, etcetera. Several days ago I could still think about the acacia blossoms in this town that gave a sense of the fragrance of bygone years, sometimes I would like to be delivered from my body, then again not at all. My soul seldom finds rest although the polyphonic white in my immediate surroundings ostensibly offered good prerequisites, suddenly observed the dirty-raw sun disk in the clear noon light, my predilection for pedantic chaos, for chaotic pedantry, my silly notions bother me more and more, anyone who comes to my place immediately comes too close to me with the question on his lips WHETHER I COULD EVER FIND ANYTHING HERE ANYMORE, those are roguish conceptions, in fact damnable conceptions. . . insertions of wood and tin, I say, scraping rasping, like in an insane asylum at night, simultaneous jumble of noises, rhythms, songs, the window panes vibrate for a few minutes, something cracked somewhere, I mean it's like a continual cracking of bones, and the storm raged like death, the storm like death—transformation birth and sickness, malice, fear, dread and many other awful things, but when the great pain comes I'll leave that point. . .

in view of the flying eye for example, I sit up in the semi-darkness, in general I often don't know what day it is, sometimes I couldn't recall what month it is, whether before or after All Souls' Day, Christmas already past? I was supposed to visit LERCH, set a date, stammered however in muddled confusion, one transvestite, little polo dog, polar dog or something! with polo shirt and wig, drunk boy drags bottle behind him, *hydrant as zebra!, the woman with the zebra gaze,* and so forth.

Two low fluttering doves crossed in a zigzag between us, I'm talking about LERCH, almost fluttered through us while we walked toward each other, we felt like real HEAD WATCHERS, thus in no time, like Goya, travel sketches in old age, the two double heads were dizzy, seeing zigzag while the eyes flicker, gray-red bird-heads and maple-heads at the window, the mountain maple, the sea eagles spur me on, but the boldness today, retrospectively, still takes my breath away, I feel exposed. Goya, the most transitory, was perhaps my father, what happened to my eyes, I don't know, or I was caught up in various delusions, my arm got into an odd twisted position when he drew me to him, and because my twisted arm hurt I told him to let me go, *one also twists an arm like that* when one wants to prove that the other person has stolen something, the hand clasps the money, why is my arm so thick? asked about the reason for my red eyes, I gave as an excuse that I had cried about some sad news last night, and with my back to the river because my feet are like a map, the image in memory shows three yarn heads on the FLY OF THE UNDERWEAR of the female child, thus infant duds, stand-up collar, crocheted underclothes, the setting for a precious stone!

The older I get the more sensitive I become, or what should I call it, there is no style in which the sought-for object could be presented, I say, the truth is, we have to leave everything up to favorable circumstances, the favorable conditions of our daily disposition, thus to CHANCE: the divinity that reigns over everything, two tender asphalt bubbles as eye breasts (Magritte), I ran around in my wobbly old flesh (fetish), the trace of an old wound, callous? wound on my forehead? actually firemark, became paler through the years, hardly recognizable anymore, like the PROTRUSION ON MY FOREHEAD, I say, number theory, magic of the mountain the forest, the bafflement of the people when they see my HORNS, my ANTLERS or the PROTRUSION ON MY FOREHEAD, suddenly, on my skull, then I finger, feign feigned the consecration, *one fingers I mean feigns a story thus one fabricates it,* like a sacrifice like an owl, am like a shepherd's child, because my throat is so thin. . .

. . . in some mountain village or another, I call, Espang Allerheiligen I don't know, with my sailor's, my flier's hat, I roam, I only rove around, in view of various observations I had made, I pondered to what extent the occurrence of particular illnesses is connected with particular geographic areas, or: whether particular geographic areas and towns produced or were conducive to specific illnesses thus poltergeists, the wound on my forehead for example, the speaker on the screen seemed to have a fresh wound on her forehead, but I couldn't make it out exactly, it could also have been small curls and clouds pulled down on the crown of her head, together with the characteristic pallor of her cheeks, the illnesses of the eye, for example, limping and loss of hair, what do I know. Carelessly (or was it predetermined?) I incurred an eye injury; when I entered a store in the mountain village after the investigation in the hospital I noticed a young saleslady who had a bandaged eye, I naturally avoided looking at her in any conspicuous way. When I returned after a few days I saw to my great horror that the bandage was gone, but so was the eye. She then had a glass eye, while another saleslady in the same store had such thin hair that one could see the skin of her head shining through, on the same day I saw girls in other stores with eye defects and loss of hair, since that time my own hair has been falling out a lot, *water vein, or I began to lose hair,* or forfeit as I had to conclude after direct observation, I searched for a word for it, I mean I've often refused to believe in such things, words fell out everywhere my hair.

To tell the truth, my head isn't with it, my hands, my eyes, my hair intertwined, a tale of woe and pity?, had a beautiful shadow now, traces of the illness. . . the traces under my hopping feet, like doves tripping along, it's ridiculous: *female genius!* old-fashioned I incline toward deafening, scalding, bleeding, injury of the eye, twisting the hip, loss of hair, I often bled easily, noteworthy enough, my mouth was dry, I call, my mouth was sown shut, my mouth was clipped, locked and ruined, without any ado, or what should I say, I'm completely wrapped up in my work but work can not always be a support, threat of bared teeth again, violent. . .

sometimes the time seems to stand still, and no one goes in or out of here, a discarded plastic bag still in the hallway, the loose tile in the stone floor now for days, jutting up, on the ledge of the corridor window and pressed against the wall, a shivering dove, the first winter storms have arrived, smoke flags blew from the chimneys across the way, icy steamer trip, how the spoons sink in the morning! the glowing hot underside of the teapot that I took from the fire momentarily imprinted a perfectly circular signet on the pink cover of the sofa, the storm now takes my leaf hut on its wings and drives it into the air, flakes in the water, the most magnificent landscapes for example in the outlines of the clouds.

In view of the flying eye, I say, I'm entirely sun, a monster, every sixty years (a fire horse), all traces of memory blurred, a reddened a rusted condition or what should I say, and in regard to JULIAN, when JULIAN says or thinks about something I sit down next to him tenderly submissive like a dove, although I direct all the days, all the minutes, who has the light, who the darkness, and because I let time run forwards and backwards, I have to think of the eternal linkage, the certain greatness, I'm also satisfied to see the hustle and bustle from here somewhat more distanced, even though it isn't possible without touching the outside world. Frankly, when I saw the small often pretty and well-kept houses and towns from the train, I felt something like a pleasant consciousness of tempo: to be able to feel security or to let the feeling arise in one is of course not primitive but rather a kind of anticipation that surprises and pleases, an emerging truth perhaps, a parable.

In signs and allusions, or in memories of a vague situation in an early time, from bobbed head on. . . soaring, circling, playing the piano in the far heights, a bird flying up (Satie), a type of flying. . . the underhead namely head pillow, gentle creaking, I put my ear to the wall of the room, hear the unmistakable sounds of someone breathing evenly in deep sleep, the whining of the dog again from below, like a screech owl at night, I occupy myself with slitting open all the pages of the book with a scissors instead of a knife, thereby the edges of the leaves become frayed, perhaps one should definitively reject the aspect of narration, Goya's donkey sequence, for example, I call, landscape in black, *pinturas negras* in Goya, the color, I call, I liked it a lot, the secret pockets had something of children's aprons. . . it's the black sun that recognized me, mild inspiration, donkey child, dove, or like a shepherd's child because the throat is so thin. . . I'll write that out IN GREEN while still lying in bed in the morning, namely with a bright green pen, or when I lie in bed without really sleeping, notice how a force turns me at intervals to the right thus turns and screws me out of bed so that it continually fizzes and bubbles out of me, *understand if you can!*

The doll sat in its gray caftan between the windows, awake, an endless moon, always lived a life of caution, privation, repressed desires, what do I know, my censer the dark pegs of human heads, guided hallucinations. . . my watch-glass window has awakened, the puffy lids, derisive laughter, raging, a breathtaking back and forth, an incessant hopping and dancing: while my need to withdraw from the world becomes increasingly urgent, I still want to extort the remaining time, press and entice everything out of it. . . have departed from the beaten track quite a bit, must artificially generate my own emotions sometimes, they often seem not to be genuinely present anymore, or whatever. Must first tap, try out, stir up everything; see whether it is possible: the joy, anger, pity for example, a surrender to the world: everything has become questionable. In a frost, then I fell down from my flying trapeze, *namely as dead-loss.*

To be precise, I repeated, only repeated things, half-heartedly joining in, with my eye always on an exit, hideout, betrayal. . . the racers straight away, not to be detained in my head.

Spooning honey from the jar, at the breakfast table, smell and taste of chicken and egg, when I open the door of my place, or in the red fabric, the skin on my chest, the quiet organs, I've become reasonable like a monkey, think in a roundabout way because everything slips away from me, out of my hands, to dismember, to spray, from bobbed head on, affinity to accidents in the household, I call, can you follow me, took refuge in substitutes, kept tabs on temporality, this continual going-to-bed and getting-up! Also because I don't see any relations anymore, namely purposes, no purpose, family purpose and family cancer ("was there anyone in your family with that disease. . .") and so forth, *finger, shooting up.*

Recognize myself with flier's hat shower cap, I suddenly have lapses of memory, turn my eyes to the left because of the tennis balls that constantly go astray, study Pasteur Goya Yoga and Freud, what do I know, thus transfigured look in the encyclopedia of heavenly truths. . . line-counter as bookmark, of course I include my daily reading material in my *writing,* I call, how else, also the letters I receive, *shameless,* as LERCH once said, presumably an allusion to my *correspondence-attack* directed at him at the time, that's all a long time ago but I remember every word: the temptation is great, that we become close to a person in letters to an extent that in no way corresponds or no longer corresponds to the personal relationship, and that happens because we give in to our favorite tendency for the act of letter-writing, that mysterious FALLING PREY to something, of which our thinking consciousness basically knows very little indeed, so that it fearfully shrinks back from a subsequent reunion with the addressee in person. . . oh, how it gets away from us, LERCH had called, how much the absorbing white of the stationery overpowers and dissolves our otherwise so strict restraint. . . I didn't immediately understand what he was trying to say, I understood ever more slowly, already at that time, or something in me resisted understanding, the beginning of all misfortune. . . I suddenly have lapses of memory again, thus interruptions in my consciousness, or what should I call it, for a week I've had severe disruptions of sleep, find myself in a painful whirl, a state of being half asleep, feel myself plagued by frightening premonitions, something could happen to me that would inflict injury, that could cause pain, in signs and allusions, in flashes of memory of a vague situation in an early time. . . visits of relatives, the two birds, the blue one and the green one, the two sons of relatives with their gifts for me: two little birds fixed in a position of nodding to each other, and when their father took their picture the boys held their ears in fright immediately after the flash bulb went off like a signal as if the flash had penetrated their ears, picture puzzle and vesper image, and I opened the wet umbrella so that it would dry out on the sofa, saw the drops run off and seep into the blanket, I saw it myself, everything dismembered and sprayed, scattered, dispersed, torn from the hands, withdrawn from consciousness, *effusive piano playing.*

It is the dusk (the demon) the cutting off, that's the scene, unfastening the arms the legs, how to live, how to live here, how to stand up to the world?

Prefer now to use my elbow because I am electrical, then I scribble something in my notebook, laugh and talk, painstakingly keep my appointments, play my role (WHICH ONE?) perfectly, read Goya monographs a long time, but let up again now, everything so fluctuating, the purest distraction, diversion, temptation, a bird sound most striking to the ear, I also come across books, or books are passed on to me *in a mysterious way,* I prop myself up on my arm when I read at night, or it goes to sleep and I freeze, irritated I fling the blanket over my shoulder, slip under it now and then, I wake up at two-thirty or earlier, with no need to sleep any more, read then until dawn, the book falls out of my hand, I doze off. . . upon waking again the view out the window, a painting-over, the most magnificent landscapes for example in the outlines of the clouds, happiness for the eye, between the shimmering clouds, the double sky has so much attraction, that is considerable, solely and literally true, the insistent figure of light, now we have a degree of heat, a winter spring it seems, everything dissolves again I mean in analogies, table and bed, or moved to a daytime scene, I smell the spring, obsessive: musk, labiatae. . . ma mère. . . polyphonic light work, *LICHTWARK* (in Goya). . . the shadows dipped in paint, shadows of great density, or the colors remained alive in the shadows, I'm talking about LERCH, that then gave the friend much color, to be on the road through the express messenger, I displayed the apples, one completely mumified, black leathered, the other wrinkled, shriveled up, the single red one, after he had washed it and dried it with a hand towel, he put it into the left pocket of his jacket, the organ of laughter at the root of the heart, the distance is welcome to me now so that it is almost a shock when he announces his coming. Earlier his departure left me in a maimed condition, as if one had removed my arms and legs, namely the Three Kings. . . come and go, in water. . .

Moved to a daytime scene, the mountains flow over from it, the eyes, as if we were suddenly washed around by a gulf stream here too, it roars so much, one can hardly hear one's own voice. NO ONE. NOTHING. When I look up, when I wake up, the date pit in the middle of the room, a pear leaf on the kitchen table, I saw someone on the street in nice clothes, later/illusionary?/ spaniel with white nurse's cap, ears presumably cropped. . .

We exchange emotive words, ZEITGEIST and SOUND OF WOMEN, L. FRENCH GRAVE (which may be an abbreviation for LENGTHENED, LEFT, LOST) IN HUMAN LIGHT, SMELL THE SPRING. . . or polyphonic LIGHT WORK (LIGHTWARK in Goya), OBSESSIVE MUSK, LABIATAE. . . MA MÈRE. . .

Eaten from the fist, I call, everything somehow illusory, for instance to think that I could now do anything other than write,

I mean the *Egyptian possibility* brushed us, but passed by quickly, Old Cairo in an inner courtyard of the Viennese steppe, or something like that, with horsetail woods, brownish figures in the fountain, an emerging truth, gradually I forgot him, still only in bundles, towering from frozen seascapes, dried reed. . .
Now everything is past, long gone, the rain, the wind, bridle of the window in the snow flakes, the colorful covering hung up, and sweeping, rinsing the street, down the avenue. . . past years. . . a god-winter. . . on the back of the dog there was snow.

I don't know anymore, I don't know anything anymore, my memory has gotten lost, my breath momentarily makes crystals, my hair stands on end, I can't focus for a long time, the green and red pens on my writing desk, red flips over into green and vice versa, suddenly the laming condition of sleep, almost fall forwards, while no one is watching, almost no one watches; I was ignorant in many things that I learned only later, too late, these changes in me how am I supposed to understand them, my feelings from before are hardly comprehensible to me anymore, last night for example, how does one's heart establish connections, the date pit in the middle of the room, two black appleseeds at its poles, solely in the second itself, I suddenly had lapses of memory so that I wished someone would turn my head or my gaze around, like that of an innocent lamb or calf, so it would become aware of specific things, *the subjugated submissive human animal.* . . so it would learn to see and hear and become enlightened in mind, sight, and hearing. . . thus me, my head turned toward the chock-full shop there in the street for example, so that I am supposed to get and carry something, am supposed to be careful of everything. . . a large bunch of flowers wrapped around me, shaking my head, my hands, familiarity of the system and the NARRATING OF THOUGHTS. . . then I hear my voice as it says something or another, *actually recites,* a neurotic relation to my sense organs, the phone booth embushed by green, my ears in the shutters, neurotic forehead eye (overbra), I hear better what I also see and vice versa, sensations of the eye, the field of vision completely rolled out, or *to see and hear with all eyes and ears.* . .

if it initially seemed to be only a temporary illness in the right ear, weeks and even months had passed in the meantime without the condition having improved, if I at first measured the time of my suffering in hours and days, soon weeks and even months had elapsed before I could and wanted to go out of the house again, if I at first reckoned with only a few days, it had meanwhile turned into several weeks even months. I usually sat by the window, looked from there down at the street, while a constant roaring in my head like the roaring of wind frightened and confused me, turned my thought-associations into turmoil, a cut and a reed of the waves, I call, sharp-edged harping grass, torn out of a terrible dream, bleeding breast. . .

I sat by the window, looked from there down at the street, I saw them sitting in front of the house across the way in the BODY, the tarring crew sat there and ate their breakfast rolls, it was actually a huge stage on which they sat, a long wooden bench on which they sat in rows, and on the back wall of the wooden box stood the word BODY in large letters, a hut, I call, embushed already by spring, in front of my window, or what should I call it, rain writer and wreath, entries on the flying intention, seen together like NIGHTINGALE AND NEEDLE.

Somehow illusory, I call, I don't know anymore what it was I remembered, perhaps the signs of aging on the back of my hands, or the look of my rotten teeth in the mirror, my sunken cheeks, and eyes, my bare head. . . sometimes I also got the times of day, the seasons confused, I got things mixed up, the names of cities and countries where I had traveled earlier, birthdays and namedays of family members and people near to me, the names of friends and of my favorite authors, or sometimes I only imagined that I got things mixed up, I mean it caused a pleasant feeling in my limbs, my head, that / so that I can rest somewhere, sometimes completely headless and helpless, saw myself as inactive, defenseless, was often not in a position to defend myself against accusations, internalized so completely the distrust that people everywhere showed me that I had trouble freeing myself from the compulsive idea that I had done wrong in this and that, etcetera; didn't know anymore how I was supposed to act in critical situations, was afraid of the necessity of bringing my voice out of me, I would rather have kept it for myself, was hardly in a position to formulate sentences anymore in awareness of the innumerable looks directed toward me, felt myself incapable of grasping factual matters, expressing requests, representing positions, and if I did overcome myself at some point I had to write down the single sentence in advance, the few sentences on my note pad in order to be able to say anything at all, also no one paid any attention to me when I made a move to say something, I mean people were not prepared for that, and made me feel it. . . all of that is however only conjecture, I call, I want to stamp my feet!

I fall on my knees, however, I fall on my knees, fall to the floor, utter prayers of thanks as soon as I have succeeded in typing a sentence, what kind of life—

sometimes I am consumed by mortal anxiety, sometimes I am seized by horror, sometimes I feel my physical end approaching, and if I didn't have this my writing, this my incessant life-preserving *writing* I would have given up long ago, I would have given up or gone insane, *I write my books as I have to write them,* I call, *undressed and uncoated: the naked truth!,* but it was a difficult course, but there are no more excuses, form and content condition each other, etcetera.

Lots of things happen to a person in the process, I mean one has no other choice, but one also wants it that way, thus we have already made progress, in comprehending very definite important things, I say, *or I am already very light, in life,* it's a long time ago I was a child and it snowed a lot, I remember, thus I reflect on value and the absence of value, beauty and ugliness and how they seem interrelated, truth and deception, seduction and finding the way, the subject matter is always unreal like the waves of the sea, over the deepest treasures, *understand if you can!*

Thereby I find it difficult to remain oriented, I call, I fall into brooding, I mean I often don't know what I am supposed to think of a situation, how I am supposed to regard events and appearances, then I don't see anything anymore, I don't understand anything anymore, remain unparticipatory and outside, prefer to keep out of it.

Or like a lost child, I long for the PROMPTER, thus for a person who tells me and prompts me in everything that I need for maintaining this my general and outer life, don't have a gift of gab at my disposal, can you follow me?

Crossed-out passages for example, I'm talking about LERCH, that's the scene, the flaming angel is open in the man, or what should I say, we sat facing each other, my gaze suddenly strayed to his crotch, glided seemingly accidentally over it, I don't know how, I came back to it again and again, but he smiled about it or he laughed it off, I ate standing up, we made love standing up, he stalked up and down in the room with me, and rejoicing with me in the flower room, up and down, had lifted me onto his feet, trotted around with me, namely on stork legs, a so-called happiness in love, there was an aviary with a swarm of birds in it, and I heard it unremittingly whizzing, an aura has power, I call, I heard it buzzing in my head, suddenly a swarm of people behind him when he appeared in public, especially younger women, half-gone days, indeed everything forgotten, lost, drifted away everything gone, life has become extensive, too extensive to allow for an overview of everything at once, the line of the horizon can no longer be made out, I've become a person without memories, or I am a person who possesses almost no memories, a weakness in seeing presumably, team of birds, accelerated event of time, a pink blooming in the garden, I don't know anymore what it was I remembered or whether I was only in the process of preparing myself for a time of remembering, my papier-mâché feet began to hold back, began to stumble, erosion of a face, I consist only of pieces that don't hang together, I call, everything has become muddled, everything decayed, destroyed, degenerate, I only need to think of my completely dilapidated CHAOTIC HOUSEHOLD, the unimaginable condition of my room, in which I can move around only in pigeon steps, actually I live only in the left-over space in my room, everywhere else completely stuffed with junk, stuff, trash, what do I know, mountains of books, note pads, strewn over the floor *or my notes, work and weave!* I lose most of my hair, am no longer master of myself, understand if you can, it's a long time ago, I was a child and it snowed a lot. . . I remember. . . *like antlers I'm going to bed now. . .*

We've almost reached our destination, calls JULIAN, now we've almost arrived, our trip is coming to an end, and sweated out, I call, now my life is almost sweated out, the endless cramp overcome, I call, no more excuses, no more tears, over the immeasurable lies that have accompanied me my whole life long, thus in fractions of seconds, I refrain from all considerations and work independently of all demands of social norms

and presuppositions, every sixty years a fire horse, or what
should I say, I leaned on, I conformed to everything, to everyone, a shameless making similar and becoming similar, in
general it always played a role in my life that I was able to lean
on and conform to, the small green backpack! I held on tightly
to my backpack, the faithful shoulder bag, the old umbrella!
familiarity of the system and the NARRATING OF
THOUGHTS. . . I conformed in order not to attract attention,
I've conformed in order not to be called on, not to be brought
to the center of attention, I've always conformed, for example
my clothes, I adapted my clothes to the surroundings, glazed
woodland and SNOWSHIRT so that I was hardly recognizable
anymore from a distance of five yards, but I'm mistaken.

The past years, I call, have demanded a lot from both of us,
you penetrated further than you yourself could have expected
into the realm of the imagination and not only that, you were
able to express the inner truth content, admittedly a gift, but it
doesn't come entirely without effort, one must keep oneself open
for it day and night, I mean sacrifice. I searched for truth for
a long time but truth conceals itself, someday I must find a way
out, or at least reflect on the course of the matter. . . suddenly
the breath-taking idea, I could move only as if *hopping in a
sack,* had for whatever reason forfeited the wonderful ability to
place one foot in front of the other, or as Jacques Derrida says:
". . . ligaments and nodes are necessary to take a step. . . ," a
memory, a digression, a pink doll's arm in the street, when a
leaf falls the world trembles, how does one's heart establish
connections, what I felt at one time I have now nearly forgotten,
the streams of attachment flow under the most disparate things,
my notes work and weave, I let time run forwards and backwards, a world-mirror stage, sun in my head, the piled-up letters
for example in the hallway that I wrote at night are not mine
anymore, but they haven't reached the addressee yet either, are
located in an in-between area, thus the last look out the lowered
window of the train compartment, no longer and not yet, untimely CUTTING OFF.

A stenographic symbol out of hair, thus a flight from, I
mean in flight toward, an awful crowing, being sick, currant-
blue in front of my eyes, a weak face, the barking from below,
an echoing bark, in me, she beats the air with her hand, he

repeats with emphasis every word she utters, she lets the big tailor's scissors slide over the smooth table top in his direction, directly toward him, pain and damnation, I start to cry in a corner, the pillow red from the bleeding of my teeth, at that time in the living room I ran around the table, on hands and knees, imitating the barking, panting of a dog, the quarrelling parents, I wanted to stop them, spare them the worst, I call, wanted to save them, imitated the barking and panting, the dog's barking from below so that they would turn their attention to me, walked on hands and knees, on hands and knees, round and round the table. . . to smother such a flame. . .

the skin of my chest bleeding, perforated, bleeding heart, the dog's loud barking from below like every evening, a barking, an echoing bark in me, to speak completely freely completely frankly: that can only turn out to be painful, pain of decline, endless moon, a landscape color suddenly in black, *pinturas negras,* shadowing of the eye. . .

Our Lady of the Journey, I say, it was lightning outside—what does outside mean?

Time is so obliterated—help, so the sun will set red behind my mountains, and eyes, and ears. . . until we all will finally have reached our destination, namely will have become *masters of forgetting* and all of us will have become *masters of memorylessness* and will have reached that most final of all final conditions thus the most final degree of our most final decline. . . (clouds of sugar, understand if you can).

We've now returned from France: on the one hand it was too long, I call, on the other hand over too quickly.

How many lives, how many springtimes, I call, will there still be?

How often will we still see the shining black branches of the cherry tree in spring, in them the siskin, larks, yellowhammers, finches?

How long will the years let themselves be extended, the annual tree rings, and continually further, further, and year for year, I look now far away, very far. Am like the moon and chosen, a bird that sits on the edge and waits, *and I don't know whether it means me or only my shadow.* The good day. . .

Vienna, November 1982 - December 1983

Commentary

The title *Night Train* inevitably recalls the jazz tune by that name, popularized by Buddy Morrow in the early Fifties but attributable to a riff by Jimmy Forrest from Duke Ellington's "Happy go Lucky Local." The association is not inappropriate, for Mayröcker's prose is porous enough to permit the osmotic passage of diverse phenomena, including a saxophonist's breakdown of the train. A more literal translation of the German title, *Reise durch die Nacht* (Suhrkamp, 1984), would be "Journey through the Night," a 'journey' that some people would undoubtedly undertake with headphones, listening to jazz or rock to pass the time.

Indeed, the sole 'event' in the book is a train trip at night, returning from Paris to the narrator's home in Austria. That night, however, expands to include a whole world and contracts to focus on a single consciousness, that of the first-person female narrator. She is the only 'speaker,' and it is through her eyes that we see the other characters. In the darkness of night, however, one does not 'see' anything; eye contact becomes I-contact, as the writer admits the reader into her own inner world. It is a virtual no (wo-)man's land: personal, subjective, and apart from the laws of logic.

i

In contrast to our conventional notions about literature and life, Mayröcker made an astonishing statement in a 1975 interview that has since often been cited: "I don't see a story anywhere; neither in my own life nor in life in general do I find any story-like phenomena." There is in fact no 'story' in the traditional sense of the term in *Night Train*, a fact that the text itself self-referentially comments on: "What narrative form can be relied upon, what narrative form is still defensible, we don't want to have a story told to us any more, we don't want to have to tell a story anymore" (61). And the author plays with the conception throughout: "One fingers I mean feigns a story, thus one fabricates it" (3, 69). Only with tongue firmly in cheek is a statement such as the following thinkable: "The next book, I say, will be a very smooth book, but this one, this one here can still be a bit outside the norm, thus unkempt, toward the rakish—wild" (57).

Mayröcker's polemic against 'story-telling' can be regarded as an outgrowth of the Austrian tradition of language skepticism, which culminated in the so-called 'experimental literature' of the postwar era. At stake is the issue of whether language is an adequate medium for rendering experience; or whether reality is instead not being insidiously distorted by the linguistic means used to evoke it. Conventional linguistic usage imposes causal connections, hierarchic order, and phychological coherence that are often absent in reality, whereby lived experience, escaping verbal formulation, remains ineffable. That predicament led many modern writers to eschew traditional forms and to experiment instead with innovative techniques such as multiple perspectives, the collapsing of temporal and spatial categories, and the simultaneous presentation of linear developments. The nearest English-language analogue of a Mayröcker text would perhaps be Joyce's *Ulysses* with its stream-of-consciousness narration. In *Night Train*, however, the narrator is female rather than male, and the text originated in a postmodern rather than a modern era, observations to which we shall return.

Memory, which on some level is mediated by language, is also called into question, for our 'memory' is always only a present-day interpretation foisted upon a past-time event, a "constricting coherence" (8, 12, 30). In recognition of the impossibility of recapturing the past, of 'remembering' in any true sense of the term, Mayröcker renounces the attempt, as the narrator emphatically asserts: "I've become a person without memories" (12, 14, 23, 37, 78; cf. 8, 20, 53, 66, 71, 72, 75). A past time is nonetheless narrated, as in Proust's *À la recherche du temps perdu* (*Remembrance of Things Past*), without however any pretense of mimetic recall, a situation that clearly requires re-negotiation of the border between nostalgia and critique. Fragments from experience and memory, dream and fantasy, perceptions, reflections, associations, and heterogeneous elements of thought and feeling are brought together in an atemporal amalgam. Levels of recent and remote pasts are superimposed on present, future, and future perfect possibilities of consciousness, as if time were an empty screen on which we project our specific interests and discrete illusions.

That obviously entails a rupture of realistic conventions, and the intent is to challenge the epistemology behind the 'given' structures. Reality is presented in the text as discontinuous, nonlinear, fragmentary, and ambivalent; and precisely this open-endedness is more central and significant than anything that can be objectively established. The work can be regarded as an intense exploration of preverbal, in part subconscious, perhaps unconscious experience, a flow chart of the energies pulsating through the body of an as yet unconstituted subject. If the medium is nonetheless language it is because a writer is bound—and liberated—by language, just as a painter is by paint or a musician by sound. The emancipation of the medium from the expectation of representing the external world frees language to express an internal reality. That distinction is itself dubious—"What does outside mean?" (4, 80). It could also be said that literature of this type is more 'realistic' than are externally mimetic forms in the sense of being true to experience, as a quick examination of the contents of one's own consciousness will demonstrate.

If Descartes could say, *cognito, ergo sum,* "I think therefore I am," Mayröcker's credo might be, *scribo, ergo sum.* Indeed, she formulates it as such in another prose work: "I exist I write" ("Ich lebe ich schreibe") in *mein Herz mein Zimmer mein Name* (1988, My Heart My Room My Name). Omitting any kind of causal conjunction, Mayröcker posits writing and living as inextricably intertwined, hence virtually synonymous. Writing is the all-encompassing form of existence that subsumes all the aforementioned modes of thought, emotion, memory, and imagination. There are numerous references in the text to writing, which is the central activity that produced this very text: "Our disappointments in life and the world are mercifully offset by our ability to write, without this writing ability we would have gone mad long ago" (50, 77). Writing becomes the means for examining the structure of human perception and the process by which the mind confronts and imposes an 'order' on the world.

Writing is presented as closely associated with reading, which entails a process of assimilating what one has read and making it one's own by re-writing it. In true postmodernist fashion, the text thus 'appropriates' other texts, which may be one meaning of what Mayröcker calls "parrot language" (7, 25, 41, 48, 59, 62, 65). A positivistic investigation of the work would reveal many references to the paintings and etchings of

Goya, that magician of nightmare. "Olympia" (14) appears not only as the then-scandalous painting by Manet (with the female figure portrayed in a position similar to that of Goya's "The Naked Maya") but also as the trademark on the author's beloved '50s-model typewriter. Further examples of reference include a text by Derrida, a Russian film, Magritte, Satie, and even personal letters. The narrator is constantly taking notes on her reading material for the purpose of incorporating it into her writing. "I never picked up a book without pen and paper in hand" (15). And, "If I like what I read then I want to have written it myself. . . I mean I insist upon having written everything myself" (38, 24). That, although heavily ironical, is simply a more specific instance of the way in which the central figure 'appropriates' all of art and nature for her purposes, indeed of the way the ego appropriates the world (although 'ego' needs qualifying definition in this case).

The activity of writing (and re-writing) is closely associated with a sense of place, which is most often the writer's home, the location of which remains unspecified but is presumably Vienna. The dwelling itself is presented as an "inconceivable mess" (21); it includes heaps of books, papers, notes, and pens which threaten to flood the place, leaving very little free space: "I live only in the left-over space in my room" (13, 21, 43, 78). That, nevertheless, is the "place of insight" (15, 19), on which the writer is so dependent. "I have to be able to forget myself completely in my writing" (34), and the dwelling represents "my writing grounds, writing abyss, which I find self-evident here at home but nowhere else" (15). Distance from there produces anxiety, as, for instance, during vacation at the "summer place": "because I had planned to let my writing rest there I almost went crazy" (15). But the writing place, her center of life, possesses an extremely wide radius: "I have come in contact with countless people, have exchanged places and seasons, but in fact I have not moved from my place of writing" (5).

* * *

The self is thus constituted by the process of writing, and although the product may be a construct, it is far from conflict-free. "In this my mental world there seems to be nothing but standpoints and counter-standpoints, I mean I take a certain standpoint and immediately I feel compelled to take a counter-standpoint, thus I waver continually between above and below, far and near, center and periphery" (41). Contradictions and mutually exclusive viewpoints exist simultaneously, for there is no privileged position in a decentered mode such as this. "Suddenly from one minute to the next we thus experience ourselves as our own INVERSE IMAGE" (61), as if the focus had suddenly shifted from concave to convex, reminiscent of an Escher print. Since paradox and ambiguity cannot be stated without self-contradiction, they are instead established in the presentation, and form becomes content as any perspective established is again called into question.

An example of this relation of opposites is offered by the "twin smells. . . alternating between acetone and bananas, the smells seemed however to blend for a few seconds, then to separate again immediately, the banana smell went with the color blue, the acetone with yellow in contrast" (57). An object-oriented focus thus gives way to a perception of properties, which, dissociated from their base, are free to serve as metaphors. Colors recur in various combinations, and whether attached or unattached to objects, they serve as emotional stimuli. Hence derives the image, "I spear up the colors" (7, 13, 14, 26), which is a metaphor for imaginative activity.

The color red, which "easily flips over into green" (2, 7, 56, 75), serves as an important structural metaphor. It is essentially a "Spanish-red or Goya-red" (2, 7) and is perceived as an exciting, passionate color, "intensifications in red" (2, 46); that leads the narrator to write the next morning "in green" (51, 71). The intensity is thoroughly ambiguous, resulting on the one hand in "flaming tongues" (48) and on the other in "I scratch myself bloody" (33, 35); or in "fresh green" (29) and "washed-out green" (19). If such metaphors have both poetic and meta-poetic signifance, as demonstrated below, the color red, along with its associative field, is one of the many elements that serve to mediate between levels.

References to Goya's works are sometimes explicit, such as the "Goya-red," his "donkey sequence" or *pinturas negras* (71, 80); the references are elsewhere more implicit, such as the phrase "swerve to the left decidedly coquette" (34, 35, 38), which possibly refers to the position of the female figure, "one of those Majas" (33, 35). The mention of *maja* and *majo* (2) early on announces one of the most fundamental of human relationships, that between woman and man, which comes up for later discussion. "Nada" (6; "Nothing"), the title of a Goya etching in his "Disasters of War" series, figures prominently as the reverse side of the writer's utopian vision, "uttermost element" (19, 24). The narrator's strong affinity for the visual artist is expressed in the outrageous conceit, "Goya is for example my father" (3, 30, 69).

Mention of the "father" creates a bridge to one of the central themes in the work, the death of the writer's father five years prior to the time of writing. The book becomes a symbol of mourning for "my poor pipe-father" (6, 8, 29), with whom the author identifies: "I have become my father, gilder of my father" (3, 6, 13, 31). The writer thus becomes a portraitist, one might say, although 'gilding' implies anything but naturalistic likeness. Daughter begets father, so to speak, creating an icon of him according to her conception. That is not a gesture of domination but the only possible authentic stance, for "who among us has looked into the heart of a father?" (33, 49). The topic offers the opportunity to explore origins: "Agent between father and mother. . . I become increasingly similar to both of my parents" (33). That obviously brings in an autobiographical element; but the relationship between literature and life is a question best deferred until the conclusion of a textual analysis.

The father's death leads to further considerations of death for the narrator who is now on the 'front line.' Reflections on time, the process of aging, and the meaning of life in light ultimately of death are central to the work. Awareness of the clock ticking gives rise to a panicky sensation: "I don't have any time at all anymore, I mean I have never had so little time as in these years, I have increasingly less time at my disposal, earlier I also never had enough time but it was not so oppressive as now" (45, 63). The writer reflects on what it means that "one grows old as a woman" (14), as opposed to growing old as a man. The desire for oblivion and the attraction of sleep, lethe, or anything that might mitigate the pain is at the same time a death wish, for in the end we all will have become "masters of forgetting" (80).

Death is the 'destination' of this 'journey,' and as such it permeates the trip. "That BASTARD DEATH actually manages to pull it off, and thus we are torn out of all connections, everything is finished for us, done and gone!" (33). The finality of death is painfully felt in contrast to the powerful force of life with its open-ended, transformative abilities: "the desire to revise everything. . . to be able to begin again now" (39). The speaker, like all of us, is caught in the tangle: "Everything has to end sometime. . . but it's too soon for me. . . this portioned-out life!" (9). Wonder alternates with protest, and that with a questioning of both reactions: "How this frail, this grandiose life is always still prolonged a bit! But still! (But still?)" (55). The text 'closes' with open questions: "How many lives. . .? How often. . . ? How long will the years let themselves be extended. . . ?" (80).

Awareness of the imminent finality leads to a more positive evaluation of the time one has, and at the center of the work stands the experience of what it means to be alive in the present. The question then becomes: "how to live, how to live here and stand up to the world?" (55, 57, 73). An idea of the absolute informs the whole, but it is never presented as accessible: "There is always a flaw in the most beautiful heavenly pleasures" (3), and "we push heavenly love as upsilon down into the abyss" (3). Even the desire for it is called into question: "Does it befit us to be or to seem absolute, when we are in truth only weaklings in matters of love" (17).

The text had early on posited "Beauty through Truth" (9, 12, 25, 41), but "truth conceals itself" (28, 43, 79) or there is at times only "an emerging truth" (48, 71, 75). The self is constantly searching, whereby the contradictions stand, side by side: "Thus I reflect on value and the absence of value, beauty and ugliness and how they seem interrelated, truth and deception, seduction and finding the way" (77, 7).

Just as there is no transcendence, there are no ethical/moral imperatives, for there is no omniscient point of view that would resolve the relativity of all cognitive categories. There is however the experiencing self, and the authenticity of its mode of being guarantees the validity of the experience. The power is in the concretion, and any abstraction would be false, for it is truly a phenomenally experienced world: "to see and hear with all eyes and ears" (44, 63, 75). There are "moments of perfect happiness" (11), and the euphoric moment is also an erotic

moment: "The beautiful seeing. . . all of that makes me somewhat euphoric also the thinking about him" (24, 22). Euphoria
and eroticism are closely linked to the imagination, as yet to be
discussed. The obligation is to the self or to life itself: "I still
want to extort the remaining time, press and entice everything
out of it" (72); that is, to live life to the fullest in the present.

That, as we all know, is more easily said than done, and the
text contains long passages of regret and remorse, faulting the
world but primarily the self. The 'journey' is, after all, through
the 'night' of life. Inscrutable fragments of experience contain
both urgent signals and obscure menaces, and the 'shattering'
stimuli arise primarily from externalized projections of internal
impulses: "threat of bared teeth, violent!" (18, 35, 38, 70). The
self feels vulnerable, since others may try to "look through me"
or even to "go through me" (34, 17) which gives rise to the
need "to go out with an eye shield, crash helmet, face mask,
visor" (54). The central consciousness functions both as nucleus
and as generator of the forces that seem designed to break it
apart. The despair reaches a nadir at three distinct points in the
text, the first of which is cited here in part: "Everything done
wrong, . . . it's all only lies. . . it's fake the way people talk
and move and look at each other and act. . . everything a lie,
one's entire past as well. . . it's all a fraud, a sham, oh if only
I could do it over again!" (22, 32, 66).

Such passages alternate with those of joy, renewed energy,
and creativity, as the self thrills in response to the beauty of the
world: "Perceiving the world so lively and fine with such rested
nerves in the morning, I say, that everything seems connected to
everything else, everything suggests an association with everything else, every network of thoughts immediately wants to be
spun out further, and other high-flying landscapes" (58). These
'connections' and 'associations' are a large part of what the text
is about. If the change in attitude from that cited above occurs
seemingly without motivation, that is only true to experience, for
our moods are often based less on the empirical factors that we
may find to 'rationalize' them than on unconscious impulses:
"One's daily disposition, which at any one time is composed of
innumerable and imponderable elements of mood and feeling,
determines the form of a text to be written" (25, 41)—and 'the

life to be lived,' one might add, given the author's identification of living with writing.

Metaphors for this life of imagination and creation are numerous; they include lightning flashes that function as "memory-lightning" (12); swarms of birds and butterflies that torment as well as incite; and "my watch-glass window had awakened" (5, 28, 51, 52, 55, 72), stimulating the imagination. Writing ('marking') accompanies living to the point of synonymity, as becomes evident in the intention "to mark the movements of consciousness in gentle ecstasy, so that I wanted to ask myself, is it paradisal?" (56). The vision is momentary, and its end is often signaled by the phrase "the dream is gone," or "dream-end," or "it's already gone again" (8, 13, 16, 17, 19, 22, 33, 38, 55, 59, 63, 64), having faded because although "I'm completely wrapped up in my work. . . work cannot always be a support" (29, 70).

Consciousness takes itself seriously, but then apparently not so: with "the organ of laughter at the root of the heart" (52, 57, 74), "I almost began to laugh about it, imagined animated animating dreams" (20). The text indeed contains elements of surrealistic humor, comic renditions of themes that are elsewhere treated seriously, with comedy and tragedy functioning as flipovers, like red and green. Examples include the woman with a glass eye (70), the sexton consulted to arrange a mass for the father (64), the drunk boy dragging a bottle behind him (64, 68), the woman with a zebra hairdo—"a most unlikely decor" (64), and the plastic sacks that weigh down the Three Kings (62)—like anvils on a hummingbird. An affinity for dogs to the point of identification with them enables the speaker to see "this outburst of laughter in dogs' faces, for example, no one can recognize it, but they laugh!" (57). Irony, particularly self-irony, is prominent, and it serves to preclude any sense of pathos or self-pity. The narrator tells of her "predilection for pedantic chaos, for chaotic pedantry" (68); and "It's ridiculous! how seriously I still take all of that" (37). The self-characterization is totally disarming and precludes any outside evaluation of person or lifestyle, which would be beside the point in any case.

The ambiguity is all-pervasive in questions of personal identity, where the many-sided figurations remind one of the spatial dissection in a Cubist painting. Psychology becomes an embarrassment in art, for all that emerges from the deep dark depths is an uninterrupted flow of words, and to break through repression would be to destroy one's mythology. The self is seen as alternating between extremes of withdrawal and involvement with the world, distance and nearness to other persons, dominance and submissiveness, attraction and repulsion, dependence and independence, active and passive stances.

In a rare moment of narcissistic self-love the speaker declares, "of all the people in the world I am basically interested in only one person and that's me" (28). More prominent is the recurring motif of self-effacement, which is often expressed in a phrase normally reserved for an angry imperative to another person, 'Get lost!.' That becomes a wish for self-annihilation for this speaker, "I want to get lost!" (7, 13, 18, 33, 43, 63). How can the reader, how does the central consciousness reconcile the inner division? Even to begin to answer, one must look at the strategem.

ii

To take the self as the topic of poetry indeed presupposes a strong sense of self. Who among us can so trust his or her impulses? Would it not be easier to define the self with reference to the outside world? Assuming the self as subject and taking that self as object means that poetic inspiration is connected to personal identity, and that interdependence has far-reaching consequences, "ramified resources!" (3).

The narrator's self-understanding often takes the form of partial identification with and assimilation to another person, for "I become increasingly similar to all the people I love" (30). The causes as well as the consequences of this process are shown to be both positive and negative, and it is further operative for both desirable and undesirable characteristics. The positing of similarity and identity with forms outside the self gives rise to an alter ego or a 'double,' as the speaker finds appearances of the self in the external world, often in mirrors and photographs but also in completely foreign objects. By a 'doubling' of the self the poet projects parts of it onto other people, particularly onto loved ones, but also onto animals and onto nature itself. On the outside the spirit lingers to inspire (or haunt, in a negative context) the writer. Having thus invested nature with her own image (and at the same time purged the self

of the demonic other), the writer can find it again as poetic
vision. Imagination, turned inside out, thus finds itself in the
world—whereby 'appropriation' indeed acquires an interesting
reflexivity. The inquiry into natural origins, "am I perhaps my father. . .
or my mother" (30) becomes also an inquiry into artistic origins;
and both become an inquiry into the nature and art of origi-
nality. The self, at least on one level, is perceived as continuous
with nature: "If one pauses a bit in the midst of this
splendor. . . one is momentarily admitted to this realm, caught
up in the web of this PRIMEVAL MEADOW" (10). The
'garden' is the spatial displacement of a temporal fixity, namely
a fixation on childhood and its attendant unity. Admission to
that realm constitues a grounding of the creative principle in an
organic sphere. Passages of pure nature description reveal a
unity of being, albeit momentary or as absence, as the adult ac-
knowledges separation from the source: "a garden the neglect
of which often touches me deeply" (4, 26). Poetry then becomes
a problem of mediation, that is, of language. But poetry cannot
become substantial until it gives up its attempt to embody sub-
stance other than itself; and to become primary it must banish
the reality that it could not capture in any case. That must
certainly be part of the author's rejection of 'story-telling,'
which in effect constitutes a rejection of reference. It also plays
a role in the denial of memory, which by definition entails an
awareness of the distinction between 'then' and 'now.' The
lifting of that distinction effects a negation of time, and the
narrator can embark on a visionary quest for origins. Given the
"many staircases in my head" (49), the quest leads "down the
stairs to a childhood home that was once my most familiar
place" (17). Then "(I) feel myself ageless, maybe seven years
old" (58), and "now I am again the astonished obedient
credulous (old) child" (20). The child exists in adult life as an
untamed side of the self which is unacceptable by societal
norms; the twin alter egos of child and 'wild' woman "can
understandably be neither interesting nor attractive for others but
rather repulsive and ridiculous" (50). Since life takes place in
time, timeless is only the condition of death. It is nothing other
than death, literally and metaphorically, that constitutes the being
of poetry.

Through a process of self-incrimination the writer 'kills off' the natural—child and wild—sides of the self, as expressed by the title of Mayröcker's first major collection of poetry (*Tod durch Musen*, 1966, "Death by the Muses"). In so doing she liberates that natural self for existence in a more safely concealed sphere, free from societal jurisdiction. The above-mentioned Dionysian desire for dissolution is never separate from a desire to return to the point of departure. The death of the natural selves provides another, less guilt-ridden self with material for poetry, as expressed in a moment of self-reflection: "Life must really be totally demolished before we can find ourselves" (20). In short, the writer exorcizes a childlike, 'demonic' self, which is socially unacceptable precisely because it is natural, and yet retains this self on a different level, which is the origin of her art.

* * *

That kind of death is closely linked to artistic creativity, and we see the wild self searching in the cemetery for an understanding of its origins: "the open grave. . . for a moment I had the feeling of standing again in front of a mirror, in which could be seen the face of my father that bore my own features" (30). Origination is crucial because priority is synonymous with authority. Just as the parents are the interiorized other on a biological level, the search on a poetological level is for antecedents that have been absorbed into the instinctual life of the self. The narrator and her partner are guided in the search by the she-wolf, who later turns out to be part of the self, but who then disappears. The inscriptions on the tombstones constitute "an unusual, arousing list" (31), and among them the narrator finds the name "Prompter," as yet to be discussed.

The quest is characteristically presented as a downward motion, a descent into the underworld: "Eyes and ears dive down in the light roof of leaves" (57, 65). "My experience of the world is comparable to falling into a funnel" (49), or "I fell down deep for a moment, then one seems to perceive the surroundings as if in a magnifying glass" (46). The descent into the grave and other subterranean regions implies a descent into the psyche, "figures in the belly of the ship and the body of the mother" (32). There the reverie takes place in a visionary timelessness. The descent is often into the 'ground,' which functions both literally and metaphorically as the place of origin and of return. If the narrow enclosure of the writer's dwelling on an empirical level implies psychic inwardness, it later becomes a "shelter in one of the old horse stalls" and "a strange shelter that hardly lets in the world. . . underground" (38). It is a quarry of raw materials, "the free hunting ground" (63), allowing for a "digging in luxury" (63). At a difficult point "I am principally groundless" (14), yet "it is the abyss that encourages me" (25, 41). After the graveyard experience the text offers a quotation: "'then you have a different ground under your feet'" (31).

The process is fearful and painful: "an open grave, and suddenly I also lost blood, suddenly I noticed the pool in which I lay and began to cry out of shame and fright" (36). "Perhaps now I should always go to bed with gloves on so that I don't scratch myself bloody in sleep" (35). The metaphor of 'bleeding' is an extension of the theme of injury and illness that accompanies the creative process. It is introduced as follows: "old-fashioned I incline toward scalding, deafening, bleeding" (3, 5, 28, 70), and further described: "That saws open my veins, makes my blood clot, ties up my abdomen, breaks open my breast, crumples my heart, dismantles my face" (18), so that "my bones hurt, teeth are lost in dream" (49).

The theme of illness and injury occurs frequently also on a more empirical level. There it is correlated with awareness of the objective effects of aging and the subjective feelings of fear and guilt. Both of those impulses are relativized by the ironic self-characterization, "a neurotic relation to my sense organs" (63, 75), and the self-critical questioning, "is the suffering in my soul?" (13). Finally, "I asked the doctor whether my illness was merely of an imaginary nature" (45). The dialectic continues and assumes a structural function as it is associated with the death of the father (and the loss of the lover). It is 'resolved' only later: "The fact that I suffered from this illness for weeks, indeed months and still suffer, I can attribute finally only to my indecision about having a holy mass held" (64). The 'resolution' is none, however, for it takes place on a satiric level. The sexton consulted turns out to be interested mainly in money (64), which reveals the narrator's attribution of cause to be highly ironic.

On a poetic level the descent is often associated with water, for "one constantly wants to wash oneself clean, to begin anew, perhaps it's a dream of humanity to realize itself in this way" (22). But, "how many cleanings (removals) are necessary until we no longer need to be ashamed of an essence" (36). The process proves to be efficacious, "these changes in me. . . noises of the water" (62), and at some points anyway "we have bought ourselves free" (22). Whereas the 'water' imagery often refers to the psychological realm, it is equally relevant in the creative realm, and the two are inextricably intertwined. On the trip "I am disaccustomed to any bright overly extravagant colors (soap)" (3, 5, 7, 26), but "at home, the best ideas occur to me during the process of bathing" (5). Then "the raven that scoops (scooped) water comes close to my bed" (52, 50), "(I) washed my teeth with an almond" (47, 58), and "emerged from the waters of sleep with the knife between my teeth" (36). "The mountains flow over from it, the eyes, as if we were suddenly washed around by a gulf stream" (74). Then "the book comes again aqueousness" (59), "a pale streak of lightning in the white water in the white glass" (67), and "I poured and poured from the bottle although the glass threatened to run over, had long since run over" (67). An angel appears that effects the transformation: "what an invention! to concede a temporary solidity to liquid substances, oh how happy we can be" (48).

On a more empirical level, the descent into the "writing grounds, writing abyss" (15) appears as a 'rootlessness': "I roam I only rove around" (4, 18, 25, 69), and "paranoid woman roaming the streets" (37). That can be regarded as an extension of the motif of the lack of domestic comfort in the writer's home, and the 'homelessness' connects it also with the 'gypsy' motif: "only notes, gypsy-like" (9), and "like the gypsies. . . when they roast the raw green beans over the open fire" (36). The lack of orientation (7, 40, 57, 77) frees one from the constraints of convention: "Sometimes. . . I got things mixed up. . . or sometimes I only imagined that I got things mixed up, I mean it caused a pleasant feeling in my limbs, my head" (76). In that disorientation provokes the search, it provides a motive for poetry: "that/so that I can rest somewhere, take hold somewhere, that/so that my foot can somewhere get a grip" (4, 6, 76).

The preoccupation with internal affairs brings with it a disregard of external appearance, and 'clothing' is also a motif throughout. On a poetic level it takes the following form: "I've always imagined a type of eternity, the neck lined with a lace collar, the lace collar turned up over the coat collar, my thin hair over that" (23, 37). The empirical level, in contrast, presents an image of a "bag lady" (28, 37) who totally neglects her appearance, roaming around in "vagabond-like travel clothes" (13). The curious neologism "overbra" (44, 63, 75) refers possibly to the correspondingly 'innovative' inclination simply to add on layers of clothing rather than changing clothes: "not unbutton anything. . . simply pull things down over it, short-cut procedure" (37). The resulting "layered look"—an ironic counterpart to contemporary fashion—suggests the multiple levels of the psychic. It is no accident that the item of clothing chosen for topicalization is associated with an erogenous zone of the body, as yet to be discussed.

'Food' is an infrequent but important motif, and it helps also to explain the 'lace' metaphor cited above. "Hectic sugary things" (7) are introduced early on as something excessive and luxuriant, like "the tongue pastries in the middle of a dream" (61). Then comes an "intense feeling of fondness for sweets. . . in a mood for nonstop nibbling, tasting, trying a bit, or tripping with guarded step into the next room to the open box of candy burgeoning with white lace paper, a mental gift" (43). The 'food' is transformed into energy: "oh this confectionary profession: I went in for sugar, was also set on fire!" (47). That is associated with "a type of eternity" (as cited above in the 'clothing' metaphor): "Went in for sugar white like in the morning light, each of the Christian worlds white like a Christ" (47), an image opaque enough to justify separate treatment later. Picking up the "lenten cloud" (22, 39), it concludes with "that most final of all final conditions. . . clouds of sugar" (80). The 'hunger' is at once sensual, sexual, and spiritual.

The time of descent is of course the night, and there is an "odor of burnt night" (12, 28) because "nature smells like burnt night" (17). The latter metaphor illustrates once again the consequences of grounding the creative principle in an organic sphere; with that as the source, there is no dichotomy between art and nature, and either or both could stand as the grammatical subject of that metaphor. The (naturalistic) cemetery visit is further joined with the (poetic) descent in the assertion, "it smells like burnt night, pine boughs, grave chamber" (11). The pain of creation, "flotsam and jetsam of the night" (36), is coupled with a strange type of pleasure, but "the ecstasy decreases with increasing daylight" (41). After covering so much 'ground' at night, the task then becomes "claiming the land of our imagination especially in the morning when a condition of half-dream still envelopes us" (45). "In all points of view it depends on whether one is shaken into position, after sleeping, and each time in excitement, or fever frost" (51). That transformation of interiority into art may be one meaning of the recurring phrase, "moved to a daytime scene" (12, 17, 52, 74).

Such images and many more are correlated with descent, which yields poetic inspiration, which leads to ascent. Directionality is a matter of entailment, as evident in the above images and further illustrated by the following: "dive and fly" (65), "something from its depths: a rising pair of wings" (48), "a bird flying up (Satie)" (71), and "flier's hat shower cap in the mirror" (51, 72; cf. 69). Those contexts illustrate also other metaphors connected with inspiration, namely birds, flying, and water, with mirrors being associated with identity. The 'flying' may entail a subsequent 'fall,' which is however not to be confused with 'descent.' Love, for example, was "like a flying and falling" (21), and "I fell down from my flying trapeze, namely as dead-loss" (72). The visionary flight, in contrast, is narrated as follows: "I fly down and up again, first down then up, together with my mother, we take off from the windowsill, watch out for the high voltage wires, actually the dream is gone, place of insight. But I have thereby gotten to know the uttermost element" (18). The speaker senses the pressure to abandon the fearsome interiority and to retreat back to reality; but she has meanwhile experienced the ultimate, the presence of death and creation.

Ascent is presented also as a forward motion, for which the 'foot' stands as metaphor—or fetish, on an empirical level. "My miserable papier-mâché feet can hardly be felt anymore" (14, 78); and "my whole foot is a stone, I gave as an answer when Julian asked me, is there a stone in your foot is there a stone in your shoe, shall we go for a walk?" (10). But then begins the warming process: "There are the fire-feet in my dwelling" (19), and "my feet smoke, the smoke was already rising, they were already singed" (8). The transformation is effective, for "I stammered foot prayers" (47), and "I wear white feet at present (sea gulls)" (43, 60, 66). "My feet are like a map" (69), and "a deep feeling of pleasure flows through me when I can use my legs my feet as before, how swiftly, how nimbly, how thirsty for knowledge they run before me, they even go up hills, without delay I want to graze on the sky" (17). The counter-images to that are "as if hopping in a sack" (79) and "perhaps crutches, substitute" (34).

The 'eye' is obviously an important image for sight and 'insight': "these two insights (inscapes) overlap" (3). "Water-clear Alaska especially the eyes" (30) leads to a "bewitching eye scan" (55, 66). It is connected with many other images, such as 'water' and 'descent': "I lie in the damp hollow of my eyes. . . the watery blue in the sockets in the eye sockets" (52). It is also erotic: "two tender asphalt bubbles as eye breasts (Magritte)" (69), which relates back to "intertwined shimmering asphalt images at night" (57). The eye is often associated with 'flying,' as the "neurotic forehead eye" (44, 63, 75) becomes the "flying eye" (58, 68, 71), "a type of flying" (43, 57, 71), and "entries on the flying intention" (58, 76).

The visual realm contains its own bridge to the acoustic, for "I see better what I also hear" (44); conversely, "I hear better what I also see" (75). Thus "the ear substitutes for the eye" (53), and the "echo effect" (5) produces "acoustic after-images" (66, 55). There are indeed many such sound images, for, "I have always enjoyed a particularly acute sense of hearing" (3, 5). The "cracking of bones" (55, 66, 68) is ambiguous and suggests something very internal, accompanied by the awareness of the presence of death; fear is expressed as "my bones are frightened" (8) and intimacy as "we often exchanged bones" (35, 50). The strange sounds are at times associated with the creative process: "now and then it demands also a stricter etching, scratching, scratching to pieces" (43); but that "to pieces" can also lead 'to death' without rebirth.

Several images have quasi-religious connotations. The "horns" (6) visible already on the child, become "antlers" (17, 43, 61, 78), with numerous references to deer (14, 25, 28, 35).

Not surprising is then "the bafflement of the people when they see my horns, my antlers or the protrusion on my forehead" (69). The speaker herself questions its origin: "the trace of an old wound, callous? wound on my forehead? actually firemark" (69). It could possibly be associated with the 'stigmata' of a saint marked by a deity. That would create a link to the "apostles" (11) and "chair saints" (36, 39).

Images of 'fire' and its associative field recur as the counterpart to 'water.' There is the "descent of the fire" (36, 37), "the burning wheel in my chest, fire wheel every morning" (27, 28, 23), the "fire salamander" (23), and the "fire horse" (71, 79); also the "glowing ashes" of the she-wolf (31). The image "the flaming angel is open in the man" (3, 46, 78) expands into "the red figures, flaming figures on the outermost edge, beautiful masks with flaming mouths. . . the beautiful masks from whose mouths the flaming tongues shoot forth, an outermost edge of the bed" (48). Hence derives the "speaking in tongues" (62), a metaphor that serves to legitimize the internal discourse of the self, as remains to be investigated. It is obviously of biblical origin, and it may also be a consequence of the motif, "upon emotional stimulation I try to endure this parrot language," as previously mentioned. Its arduousness stems from the fact that "the language of the other side is hard to learn" (68).

There are repeated references in the text to 'messages' and diverse modes of communication. These range from "pneumatic dispatch" (51, 53), "messenger bag" (58), "red signal flag" (55), and "signal giver" (55) to "receiver and transmitter" (55). There is the zebra that "seemed to want to reveal some sort of secret" (62) and the speaker "in search of something. . . some kind of promise, news, a coded message" (65) or "notice, message, and announcement" (63). These "signs and allusions" (71, 73) lead to the assertion, "every sentence should be a message" (53, 64, 65) or a "parable" (71, 15). The nature of that 'message' comes up for discussion later. It may, for example, refer to this very text; but that is again relativized by the narrator's derogatory tone: "one cannot expect acclaim for that kind of prayer fantasies" (65). Creativity is thus presented in the quasi-religious context of "saints," "speaking in tongues," and "prayer fantasies." Poetic power is such a strange phenomenon that the narrator attributes it to outside sources: "If I have succeeded in writing one sentence, a series of sentences, I fall on my knees, thank and pray, flow away in humble prayers of thanksgiving, prayer fantasies, because I never believe I can accomplish anything on my own" (15, 47, 65, 77). That the religious concepts are not to be taken literally is indicated by, among other things, the phrase "I am not certain in matters of faith" (38, 43, 44). The locating of creativity in a religious sphere can be regarded as a desire to redeem its source. Since creativity is a mystery and necessarily remains so, religion is used as a means of converting dubious origins into glorious ends. Finally, the text opposes itself to the search for 'origins,' for the origin lies at a place of inevitable loss. The text snickers at the solemnities of the chimera, for at the entrance stand the animals: "The little monkey the little lamb the little screech owl wait outside, our lost children" (22, 8).

The allegedly external force is what writers have traditionally called the 'muse,' a female spirit that inspires the male artist. But where does that leave the female artist? The myth is called into question in this text: "We have to leave everything up to favorable circumstances, the favorable conditions of our daily disposition, thus to chance: the divinity that reigns over everything" (69). The phrase, "my notes work and weave" (78, 79), bears a suggestion of the Greek Fates or Goethe's *Erdgeist* (Earth Spirit), a natural force that takes its own course. By framing the self as the organ of that omnipotent 'chance' or 'weaving,' the text demonstrates that in the end one is oneself the only 'muse.' Creative power proves to be lodged in human personality, ambiguously posed between its divine and demonic heights and depths.

Such passages can be regarded as metapoetic commentary on the creative process, and the resulting poetry contains its own theory of poetry. Indeed, the container and the contained, as inside and outside, are often interchangeable, or rather, co-existent. The narrator's laconic comment, "there are indeed very different levels of reality" (22), refers certainly also to the text itself, and the multiplicity of levels on which any given statement operates accounts in part for the complexity of the work.

The literal night, for example, provides access to the hermetic region of sleep and dream, which is a prelude to creativity; and the resulting product of that process entails an exploration of its own presuppositions. Anguish about the facticity of death and its likelihood on a literal level alternates with a desire for death and the ensuing inspiration on a poetological level. The borders of the ego are closed off to prevent outside interference; and they are opened again to permit the descent that leads to poetic flight. The fluctuation in borders enables the projectability, receptivity and transformability of the self; but it also entails an attendant instability and ambiguity in one's sense of the self and thus of all else as well, as humorously reported: "today about seven o'clock I was what I really am for a moment" (13).

iii

That degree of interiority involves no bypassing of empirical reality; on the contrary, both sides are enhanced by the mutual resistance. An important topic of the entire text is, "the strong friction between the soul (our souls) and the outside world" (18, 28, 65). The latter includes "people. . . who repel by attracting me and attract by repelling me" (28). Although those 'people' are not individualized in the text, the discussion below focuses on some of the figures (more or less) outside the self.

The mysterious figure of the "Prompter," although at times seemingly synonymous with an outside person, may be regarded as another side of the self. As a type of 'superego,' the Prompter gives guidance for living in society, as the speaker describes: "Like a lost child, I long for the Prompter, thus for a person who tells me and prompts me in everything that I need for maintaining this my general and outer life" (77; cf. 40). That "general and outer life" is not poetry but rather society. The need for a 'prompter' arises from the fact that "my mouth was sown shut" (70; cf. 21, 57, 64, 76). The speaker does not have a "gift of gab" (14, 77) but rather a "sinewy throat" (62) and is "like a shepherd's child because my throat is so thin" (58, 65, 68, 69, 71). The absence of 'voice' gives priority to writing, that is, to poetry.

If poetry may be regarded as analogous to the biblical 'speaking in tongues,' a gift of the 'Comforter,' the Prompter may be associated with the 'Discomforter': "I have brought you the Discomforter and so forth, says Julian. . . I press him, who or what is the Discomforter, does he or it possess human form?"

(21). The Prompter functions as the ironic reversal of an omniscient force. He speaks in banalities (3, 68), and the speaker often resists his practical, 'rational' advice (4, 26). The cemetery experience of finding the name of the Prompter inscribed on a tombstone liberates the speaker from the strictures of "general and outer life."

Presupposing a link between creativity and procreativity, the narrator hypostatizes her children, James and Susanna. They are, of course, also projections of the self, in this case, sublimated parts that no longer exist as such. Their primary characteristic is 'absence,' and the speaker grieves over the loss: "Where did my children, where did my baby teeth go?" (13), with the object of loss subtly shifting from other to self. The images associated with the children, the male child as well as the female, seem to be images from the speaker's own life: "oh the hair of my children, smelled like nuts, or metal" (10). The curious metallic metaphor refers to aging, which includes "a dry mouth, a taste of iron" (10).

The 'children' most often represent the speaker herself as a child. The image of 'nut' may form a link to "the date pit in the middle of the room" (4, 50, 53, 74, 75), "the small pointed stones in the berries" (15, 17), and other types of 'seeds' and 'leaves': "on the table lay a peach seed, half a nut and a leaf from a cherry tree all of which I loved very much" (13; cf. 16, 75). That connects with other types of 'fruit' as natural images from childhood; and those images now excite and inspire the adult poet: "a lemon lies on the table: a beauty! it lies there, I say, as if it wanted to prepare itself to be painted, and as my fingers clasp it I am reminded of something" (6).

Another and rather curious image from childhood is the following: "Then he tore up some scratch paper outside, and I felt it in my body as if someone tore apart my innards and heart" (13). The image is of course one of damage and destruction—of poetry and of a self. It is repeated in the present tense, ". . . I feel it as pain in my whole body. . ." (23), which gives indication of how near childhood is: "There must have been a different me at one time" (48). The 'doll' is maimed; but in its "wretched doll's skin" (34), it can depict a mood even in later life: "a renewal (memory) a digression a pink doll's arm on the parquet floor" (59, 79; 23, 29, 71). Other images of childhood

include "infant duds, stand-up collar, crocheted underclothes, the
setting for a precious stone" (69). The unity is presented as
"children's apron. . . then everything comes as easily as
children's shoes then everything fits easily together" (47, 105).

Although the death of the children is initially attributed to
a train wreck (2), it is later described as follows: "I saw how
the two children leaned against the unkempt overgrown bushes
bordering the road. . . how they pushed and shoved each other
into that thorny thicket and how they seemed to sink into it
screaming, while blood sprang forth on their arms and legs"
(63). Those children perhaps represent an earlier stage of the
speaker who describes the self as "tangled up in thorny bushes"
(26), and "flogged torn apart in the thorny bushes" (28). The
loss of childhood in this case means an internalization of it, as
"a wild bramble bush grew out of my mouth" (27). The image
is one of 'nature' emanating from the poet's body and through
the poet's voice.

An androgynous element is present too, for the speaker has
looked at sexuality from both sides: "The bearded woman at the
crossroads, AIR GAL, now and then a woman with a beard like
a burial woman from the underworld led me somewhere toward
home.. . . The burial woman possessed female and male gender
characteristics, leaned over me while I slept. . . she was a czar
(czarina), can be a pearl in my life, or a team of birds, is it the
glow of both genders?" (62-63). Attributes such as 'beard,'
'pearl,' and 'underworld' (i.e., 'foreignness') connect the image
with a number of others: "Assyrian with pearl necklace and
beard" (26), "the Egyptian possibility" (75), the "black headscarf
of a Turkish widow" (48), and "a manuscript decorated with
jewelry and brothers" (20, 41). The phrase, "can be a pearl in
my life" (46), occurs in a complex image of the father that
conjoins photography and inner vision.

The 'beard' is commonly associated with the father: "my
father. . . is shrouded in beard and woods" (8; cf. 47). And the
'burial woman from the underworld' is further delineated as
follows: "like a Christ figure she lay in the middle of the bed,
her crying children right and left, a boy and a girl, the one child
like a nut like James in ecstasy" (63). If the speaker identifies
herself with the children, as discussed above, the 'bearded
woman' is the father, who is seen as a type of "Christ figure."

There had been a suggestion of that also in the cemetery scene: "the Christ Child in his upper body" (31). The function of this figure "from the underworld" who "led me somewhere toward home" is apparently to mediate the transition from life to death. The speaker at another point hears the voice of the dead: "He calls me to him" (9), "he told me he wanted to take me to him soon" (31), and there are throughout "voices" (45, 53). The central figure in the constellation remains intentionally vague, a cross between male and female characteristics, natural and supernatural forces, and Christian and pagan myth.

The ambiguity of sex roles is evident also in that many of the views assigned to the male or female are interchangeable. For example, the female speaker reflects on a conversation with the man: "I held back, preferred to keep things to myself" (2); later the man admonishes her with nearly the same words: "You should control yourself, keep things to yourself" (25). The 'criticism' leveled by the man is an externalization of the woman's self-criticism, as illustrated by the following dialogue. He: "You can't go out in that gear. . . what will people think!" She: "With that he had touched a sore point, perhaps even the sorest point" (34). When she says to him, "You penetrated further than you yourself could have expected into the realm of the imagination" (79), that is precisely what *she* has done, in this work, for example. 'Our' gender roles prove to interpenetrate in intricate and enigmatic ways.

* * *

The dichotomous sides of the self are paradigmatically illustrated by the narrator's relationship to two men, Julian and Lerch. Who are they, or who is he? The lack of specificity allows the speaker to endow the figures with her own imaginative possibilities. "It's often hard to say where JULIAN STOPS and LERCH BEGINS, or the other way around, the two figures sometimes seem to be connected, their delimitations uncertain" (24). The fact that one of the names suggests *Lerche*, the German word for the songbird *lark*, already loads the equation; and early on the narrator identifies the other figure, speaking of "my Prompter also called Julian" (3). But then again: "The borders are fluid, the outlines dissolve, I often don't know anymore where it begins and ends with you or Lerch" (66). It is neither necessary nor fruitful to try to separate the two figures.

A 'ménage à trois' is a frequent configuration in Mayröcker's prose works, but it commonly comprises one male and two female figures, as in *Das Licht in der Landschaft* (1975, The Light in the Landscape) and in *Die Abschiede* (1985, The Farewells). If the doubling in that case can be seen as another instance of the speaker's projection of an alter ego, the doubling of the male figure in the present work may conversely be regarded as two sides of the same figure, for "I taste the change of perceptions, recognize their natural progression, see everything as possibly superimposed on everything else" (56) or "like multiple exposures of a photographic film" (50). The traditional conception of character is, in any case, rendered inoperative, since personae are used mainly as props for setting up perspectives, and perspectives function as instruments for exploring a many-textured world.

Any apparent solipsism of the imagination is counteracted by the role assigned to the male figure, a role that demonstrates the non-self-sufficiency of the single self. The male-female relationship is topicalized at the very onset, where it is seen as definitive for the reportedly regrettable course of events during the preceding stay in Paris: "Nothing worked out, least of all with each other since our relationship had exhausted itself" (1). If the problem then seems to disappear for a while, that is only ostensibly so. It is sublimated into art forms and tracked by metaphors that are later revealed to have sexual associations; for example, "momentary stove" (11, 39), "on stork legs" (5, 48, 78), and "houses walking on stilts" (24, 26, 29), an image that was associated also with the father.

The submerged realm of sexuality 'resurfaces' before long as the speaker descends further into sleep and into the psyche. The male figure is virtually the only 'Other' (beside the narrator) who has a voice in the text. The narration of direct speech, among other things, distinguishes that figure from other characters, who are described in the third person. This 'second person' stands in close proximity to the speaker, and the dialogue between the two and their reflections on the nature and experience of human relationship permeate the entire text. At the very center of the book in terms both of pages and of significance stands the memory of "unrestrained passion" (39), a memory of how "our love had been a harmony that redeemed all else, a unity that resolved everything, uttermost element" (24). But the intent of the author is not to tell a 'story,' much less a 'love story,' and language moves all chronology onto the single plane of the printed page and the present time.

Initiation and dissolution of the love affair are throughout inextricably intertwined, from "when we saw each other for the first time!" (40, 23) to "I had to assume that his withdrawal was final" (45). Time is suspended as the intensity creates an eternal present: "We've always known each other, since time immemorial. . . oh we've known each other forever" (41). Time is operative again as reflection reflects on itself: "Everything so far, so far away. . . hardly imaginable anymore" (37). The speaker asserts that "gradually I forgot him" (75); but the reverie in the middle of the night shortly after the graveyard scene speaks of anything but 'forgetting.' "The watchman has given up" since "the emotions from earlier swelling up and down don't concern him anymore" (37); and that leaves the gate open for sexual fantasies. If the speaker had earlier identified herself with "one of those Majas" (reclining nude female, as previously mentioned), she at this point posits a "masculine swerve to the left" (38).

Even the descent into the self, which is necessarily solitary, is affected by this 'Other.' That figure operates then not from the outside but from the inside, as libidinal drives are associated with poetic power. An extended image provides an example: "Lerch. . . had a face like milk and blood" (35), whereby 'milk' could be associated with childhood and 'blood' with creativity; as attributes of Lerch, both are connected to sexuality. When that is expanded to "milk and blood, an open grave" (35), the metonymic addition brings the father together with the lover. Death is thereby associated with sexuality as well as with creativity, and biological origins are joined with poetic origins under the sign of sexuality. A further example is provided by the branches of a "box-tree" at the gravesite when Polly "with a tear-stained face reached for the box-tree branches and took them and pressed them to her" (30); later "he, Lerch, hurries past me. . . a shudder in me, a long feeling of arousal, flowers on the edge of the flesh, as if he had touched me with consecrated box-tree branches" (57). The speaker associates the image "the flaming angel is open in the man" with the father; for as the 'I' sees a photograph of a man "in flames, (it) reminds me a little of pictures of my father in his youth" (47). The image is repeated verbatim in a sexual context: "I'm talking about Lerch, that's the scene, the flaming angel is open in the man. . . my gaze suddenly strayed to his crotch, glided seemingly accidentally over it. . . a so-called happiness in love, there was an aviary with a swarm of birds in it" (78). Birds, which are throughout associated with creativity, are associated also with sexuality, as evident from the preceding quotation; also "under the bird string, the most passionate times" (38), "deadly orgasm brain aviary" (37), and the origin of the image "on stork legs" (78). Perhaps those are some of the meanings entailed in the following ostensibly innocent formulation: "At that time, with Lerch, I call, ran down the steep garden path, to the frozen pond" (62), and "we ran a long time, always in a circle around the frozen garden pond" (67).

As "my thoughts coil their knots more tightly around me" (60), the speaker ponders her former 'dependence' on her partner: "I leaned on him, didn't keep my head, a kind of absence of consciousness" (21, 66). Perhaps that kind of self-surrender is analogous to the reading experience mentioned just prior to it: "I must still be very careful not to become fully involved with the book and finally disappear in it altogether" (19). It is expressed in the following image: "There are also the windmill wings that already lay me contorted at your feet again. . . Spanish is proud thus let me lie there" (54). Intimate love scenes are followed by the tension of what might be crassly described as 'sexual politics': "We often got into a stalemate in later years. . . gloated over the weaknesses that became apparent in the other" (40). 'Love' becomes an ersatz for 'absence': "If our children had lived, then now at our age we would not have to love each other instead of a child" (40). Such considerations serve to illustrate "how easily how unexpectedly love flips over into its opposite" (44).

The loss of the lover and the loss of the father are conjoined, as the speaker gives as the reason for her withdrawal from the world first the one (44) and then the other (64) and finally both or neither (75), viewing the unease as part of the existential condition itself. The "firemark" (69), reminiscent of saintly stigmata, can be associated with the "pockmark" (61) from a lover's kiss: "his farewell kiss made a black mark on my cheek" (60). Both 'marks,' the mark of creativity and the mark of sexuality, are closely related to "bookmarks. . . like life-marks" (65, 72). Sexuality, death, and creativity (schematic: lover, father, and self) are linked on a number of different levels and constitute the "basis where everything comes togther" (34, 40). Yet even that, like everything else, is thoroughly ambiguous, and it also has connotations of destruction (23,37).

* * *

There is frequent reference to the body, even in the train: "as the light suddenly went out and my eyes were not useful for anything anymore. . . there still remained the consciousness of my body" (4). The text also contains many allusions to cognitive categories, such as "brain branches" (20, 21), "brain aviary" (27, 37), "cognitive system" (28), and "mental world" (41). The phrase, "my mind, the dominant part of the soul" (16, 37), indicates a dominance of the rational faculties over the spiritual (thus precluding any 'cult of the dead,' for example); it however says nothing about physical being. In general there seems to be no dichotomy between the mind and the body, except in the conventional sense, as when "my doctor advises me to pay attention to my health. . . go swimming!" (32). In many instances the mind/body relationship is one of co-operation; and since rational categories have been abundantly illustrated in the previous discussion, the following continues with the physical.

The important role played by the body is illustrated by statements such as the following: "I did it with my entire physical being" (45, 67), "my body learned it even before my mind" (1) and "the body itself knows best" (63). Judging from her outward appearance, which reveals a self-willed neglect, "some people grant me only a phantom body" (16, 32, 41). The body is however highly sentient and is constantly perceiving sights, sounds, and smells, which are linked to the imagination: "Certain movements of my body seemed to elicit blinding lightning flashes" (8), "fireworks as it were, a system of electrical sparks" (19). The "meridians that flow through my body" (59) reveal the close link between sexuality and the imagination.

The language of sexuality is often heavily encoded, and although many of the phonological correspondences are lost in translation, the text moves easily from "filly" to "phalli" (14, 25), for example. Language itself does it: "a furious copulation namely with words" (52). The writer's pens and pencils lead to reference to penetration: "the maddening compulsion. . . to drive a sharp object through my eardrum" (7). The following image is one of the most graphic depictions of the 'devastation' of the sexual and creative experience: "I open my mouth wide and an enormous sun-eclipsing, raging angel in black-claw attire breaks open the two white snake eggs in my red-palate mountain range with its sharp wing blades, whereupon my revenge fills itself momentarily with a greedy tangled viper's brood that threatens to smother me so that I vomit blood" (7).

'Writing the body' has become a common concept in feminist studies, and to explore what that term may mean in this context, it is useful to consider the style and structure of the work. The stylistic form may be characterized as visionary, obsessive, and hypnotic, for the sheer intensity of the experience entails a partial loss of consciousness, as stated early on in a type of preview: "I am literally dying to write in a hallucinary style" (3). It is a voluntary submission: "(I) look back again and again in order to let this passionate color affect me once more" (26). The tension in a text that has no plot is textural rather than temporal. It is structured by images that operate incrementally to form chains of allusions, resulting in extremely rich cross-refences. A motif may be initiated seemingly unobtrusively, and it then recurs in various contexts, each time with accrued implications. After having amassed a chain of associations it at some point goes spiraling to a climax: "something. . . that intensifies at particular points to a spark-emitting spherical ball" (59). The narrative breaks off, and the motif reverts to dormancy; it may, however, spark off other motifs, or it may itself be reactivated and participate further in some larger complex. The structure is more spatial than temporal, and it could be described as a linkage of clusters—"'ligaments and nodes'" in the text that Mayröcker cites from Derrida (79)—or "the eternal linkage" (71).

Recent work in literary theory suggests a connection between textuality and sexuality. That does not come as a surprise, since the erotics of reading, like the erotics of other aspects of life, arise ultimately from the desires and pleasures of the self as a sexual being. Further, the Mayröcker equation of living with writing operates reflexively, allowing everything that is said about writing to be applied also to living. In terms of beginnings, middles, and ends, the linear 'masterplot' of traditional narration is a male mode of activity, in that it builds up to a climax followed by rapid resolution. In contrast, the rhythms and dynamics of female sexual—and textual—experience are very different. The varying manifestations of male/female sensibilities can be sought in areas such as incipience, association, repetition; inclusion, accretion, recurrence; and closure—or absence of such, since closure is not only not sought but also assiduously avoided. The text is thus 'gendered,' but less by virtue of its content than by its form.

The structural (and sexual) center of the work occurs in the second and third quarters, where the imagery reaches a maximum density, corresponding to the deepest levels of sleep or of the subconscious. Clock time is registered: "it's two thirty-four in the morning" (5), then "it's three" (12), "now it's three-thirty" (34). That is the last that the speaker looks at the clock, and the next assertion leads into the center, "can't sleep any more, the night seems endless" (34). Shortly thereafter comes the intensive engagement with the memory of love and the fusion of that with the immediately preceding scene of death. The final quarter of the work, when "waking experiences mix now increasingly unhindered with those of dream" (61), evinces a movement toward the surface, toward the day. That brings with it the safety of the quotidian, as "I sit up in the semi-darkness, now the night is almost over, the journey completed" (65). The more discursive tone and the increased instance of humor in that section bear witness to the 'therapeutic' effects of the nocturnal process.

The spatialization or 'geometrization' of a temporal process results in no de-dynamizing of the poetic object. The arabesque serves rather as a counterpoint to embellish the nonlinear process that continually circles back on itself. The empirical development is completed at the onset of the text: "We've now returned from France" (1); the cognitive and emotional development, in contrast, reaches its maximum intensity at mid-point. The end only brings it to completion, when "we've almost reached our destination" (78). Thus the beginning and the end are symbolically fused, which may be one meaning of letting "time run forwards and backwards" (17, 71, 79).

As in music, there is throughout a precarious equilibrium between theme and development, that is, between an ever richer expression of the subjective feeling and its objective working out in the form itself. The text comments on its own pace: "Like in a dream, I say, when one can't seem to get away although one moves forward at a high speed, in entirely unhampered language, right after that everything formulated very carefully and precisely again, changes in tempo" (55). The temporal structure is again conceived in spatial terms: "indications of a hypnotic future where everything seems to be driven out onto the smallest possible contact area" (59). The structure itself functions as a metaphor for the semantic meaning; and with ironic brashness the speaker 'parrots' a truism: "Form and content condition each other etcetera" (77). That 'conditioning' effect of form and content, indeed their relationship of mutual inclusion, is the topic of the following section.

iv

If past and future belong to the realm of nonbeing, the present stands as an 'in-between' area. To focus on that area entails first a look at the borders, at the world as "spherically flattened at its poles" (37). There are many references in the text to pairs of opposites; besides those already discussed one could list metaphors that are often joined by alliteration or assonance, such as "seen together like nightingale and needle" (58, 76), "vow and victory hands" (10), "apostles and airplanes" (11), and "entrance and appearance" (51). Between such clearly polar phenomena, also known as "polo dog, polar dog" (68), there is the ambiguous 'in-between' area, which represents the span of life, of sexuality, and also of narration: "The in-between tale still legitimate. . . like under hypnosis" (54). The ironic understatement which frames life as simply an interval emphasizes its transitional nature.

That region is illustrated by the crossovers already discussed, such as hybrid forms and androgyny, and also by reference to "threshold" (10), "crossroads" (62), and "a letter from Lerch,

Indian, Chinese, inbetween Mongolian" (61). It is paradigmatically illustrated by the following scene: "the piled-up letters. . .
that I wrote at night are not mine anymore, but they haven't
reached the addressee yet either, are located in an in-between
area" (79). That is also the area of art: "something iridescent
between major and minor keys" (61). It is also the duration of
the trip, as viewed near the end in the approaching 'dawn': "the
last look out the lowered window of the train compartment, no
longer and not yet" (79), "thus a flight from, I mean in flight
toward" (79). And it is also the duration of the 'stay,' whereby
the text repeats its opening statement to give an assessment:
"We've now returned from France: on the one hand it was too
long, I call, on the other hand over too quickly" (80). The poles
are represented by the "defenseless nakedness of being born and
dying" (12) and the limits of the "continual process of destruction and beginning again" (3); the 'in-between' time is then the
realm of change: "inexplicable world transformations" (56).

These 'transformations' are effected by means of metaphor.
Since "the subject matter is always unreal like the waves of the
sea over the deepest treasures" (77, 7), and further since "the
subject matter knows no limits" (3), the object of reference is
transformable; and metaphor raises it exponentially to a higher
power. The speaker sees "disguises, or models" (24, 33), and
comments laconically, "there are indeed parallels" (16, 37). The
text offers its own metaphor for the form: "That proliferates. . .
like a leg-of-mutton sleeve in the mirror, that escalates, gets out
of hand, hardly comes to a standstill" (42); until finally, "everything dissolves again I mean in analogies" (74). And metaphors
are, after all, 'analogies.'

Making connections and associations is the activity of
poetry, for which nature serves as stimulus: "Morning sparkle
outside, everything full of allusions" (39). Some of the seemingly elusive images can be seen as secondary manifestations of
primary phenomena that are narrated elsewhere in episodic form.
For example, the image "two little birds fixed in a position of
nodding to each other" (73) is possibly an "after-image" of the
relationship of the two lovers: "we stand as it were on facing
balconies and wave to each other continually" (42). Analogously,
when: "I put my ear to the wall of the room, hear the
unmistakable sounds of someone breathing evenly in deep sleep"

(71), it is probably a memory of "this your familiar breathing next to me, although it basically challenges me to breathe in the same rhythm" (16).

The awareness of loss manifests itself in a number of different metaphors that deal with the burden of memory. The ostensibly isolated image, "drunk boy drags bottle behind him" (64, 68) bears some similarity to the mushroom episode (52), which involved a third person but one whose attributes are apparently readily transferable to the lover: "and that with the mushrooms, I say, drags behind me like a tow, I say, he. . . I'm talking about Lerch" (24, 52). If the 'dragging' is the painful memory of a meaningful experience, it also manifests itself as follows: "the hem of the coat bunches up and drags on the ground" (46). It also connects with the episode of the 'Three Kings,' particularly with the odd-man-out: "One of the Three Kings, the handsome Moor, trudged with flat feet over a snow path, the two plastic sacks that he carried like weights seemed to pull down his arms, threatened to stretch them out to great lengths" (62). Those 'weights' appear at the very beginning of the narrative, where the speaker gives the reason for her restraint in the dialogue with the Prompter: "I wanted to ask more about current world conditions but that would have led too far afield: I noticed that by the lead weights, the ridges of my questions, in the folds of my gown, thus I held back" (2). The "lead weights" in the gown, the "weights" on the arms, the "hem" of the coat, the "tow" of the mushrooms, and the "bottle" of the boy are the load of care resulting from the death of the father and the loss of the lover.

What is the point of such 'recycling' of imagery? The text itself raises the question: "Why do the same memory sequences continually recur?" (49). That happens particularly "after the departure of a landscape" (49), that is, after a disturbing event. The speaker is highly aware of the process: "Certain daily tasks are always accompanied by the same memory images" (49), and "certain dreams repeat themselves, I dream for example again and again that I have lost something. . . I can also order dreams" (31). The 'playback' mechanism functions as follows (in this case in regard to the dissolution of the love relationship): "years, decades later I always still played back what had happened, unrolled everything hundreds and thousands of times before my inner eye, tested my feelings anew during these situations that were repeatedly conjured up" (42). Recurrence contributes at one point to the sense of despair: "Everything a sham, everything made up, everything recycled, reeled off, played out in all variations" (32).

Repetition might indeed be cause for despair if it were a meaningless circularity, but that it is not. The difference can be demonstrated by viewing initially a negative example: "Because we have become so similar to one another, I can expect from them, and they from me, only the eternally same stories, I mean we continually tell each other the same stories, which has made us into boring people, most of all for each other, I say, and has a paralyzing effect on my mental powers" (33). That serves as a counter-example to what is meant by recurrence. A more appropriate understanding might lead to a Nietzschean sense of "Eternal Return"; that is not an unwelcome association, but neither can one enigma be explained by another.

Recurrence stands in a curious relation to memory. On the one hand, it presupposes memory, since otherwise one would not recognize the recurring manifestations. But repetition is also a dialectic that transforms its source. Since memory is by definition in relation to something past, it entails an awareness of 'loss.' A creative recuperation of that loss means 'letting go' of what it was at that time and allowing it to change and develop. The process is similar to that described earlier for the 'death' of the self and the 'birth' of poetry. Memory must banish the reality that it could not capture in any case: "and no more looking out the rear window of the moving train" (22); that 'forgetting' allows the past to arise on other level. Memory thus embodies its own negation and leads to a transformation of 'absence' into 'presence' in a series of unceasing metamorphoses. The 'memory' is thus not of a fixed entity but one whose identity is constantly changing, like personality itself, being integrated ever anew into the ever-new present. Perhaps that kind of 'letting go' of the past is part of what is entailed in our becoming "masters of forgetting" (80).

The "repetitive mechanisms" are a "principle of repetition culled from life" (61). The narrator finds it in the organic sphere, the source of being: "The contours of the mountains. . . seemed to imitate one another in various layers and shadings of gray-violet, each hilltop imitated the one above it, as it were, and so forth continually, in five or six rising levels, similarly the hollows replicated themselves down to the flatter dips, so that one involuntarily had to think of an intertwined canon of tones whose echo seemed to adjust itself to the movements of one's own body" (56). That the 'adjusting' is on the part of the subject rather than the object is recognized, and the narrator can apparently also control it: "Then I lowered the image half way, namely the lid" (56).

The circling back on itself represents an attempt to understand a situation and make sense of the complexities of life. "Perhaps life has become too extensive to allow for an overview, I say, perhaps the motives are stored somewhere, but fog has moved in, the line of the horizon can no longer be made out" (12, 78). The technique of processing and reprocessing represents an effort to cut through the 'fog' and to get to the 'motive' behind the appearance. Repetition distills the 'essence,' which then crystallizes, resulting in "an emerging truth perhaps, a parable" (71). Before examining the 'perhaps' of that 'emerging,' it must be clear that the technique of repetition is a metaphor for the search for 'truth.'

That search is expressed in phrases that run like leitmotifs through the text: "in the interest of truth" (7, 11, 22, 25, 38, 68). How strong that desire is, is revealed by the fact that 'truth' is given precedence over 'beauty': "Beauty through Truth" (as previously discussed). 'Truth' is thus taken as the desideratum and 'beauty' regarded as a by-product. That even led to a change in the mode of writing: "Thus far my life has been a matter of revealing and exposing, my writing in contrast a matter of concealing and distorting, but now the techniques are reversed, or aligned with each other" (16). If the earlier dictum had been, 'Truth through Beauty,' then anything beautiful must also have been true. But since "now the techniques are reversed," anything true is also beautiful. Art thus becomes a search for truth, with beauty arising out of the imaginative possibilities of the search. The 'reversal' or 'alignment' gives priority to the existential over the aesthetic side of the equation of living and writing.

The desire for 'truth' gives rise to the sensation of everything as perhaps "somehow illusory" (22, 53, 74, 76) or "illusionary" (74); "all of that is however only conjecture" (2, 5, 12, 13, 20, 21, 25, 36, 40, 50, 62, 77); "my notes only imagine things, not all of it is true, or I only invented it" (24, 32, 40, 50); "I was caught up in various delusions" (26, 47, 69; cf. 37, 39, 41); "I've let my life pass by like a dream" (24, 32); "one is more inclined to take a dream for reality than the other way around. Although there are also such moments!" (11); "there are no witnesses but it's true I mean I perhaps dreamt it like everything else" (35, 41, 50, 64). The very avowal of its truth value, as in the preceding quotation, has the opposite effect. The generous sprinkling of page numbers demonstrates how thoroughgoing the epistemological skepticism is: "Everything too vague, here and there still points, recognizably clearer places that might offer clues to other fixed points. . . a shadowy something that momentarily seems to approach a tangible level of memory but disappears as soon as we attempt to grasp it, thus I could scarcely attain certainty" (12).

The skepticism is also thoroughly ambiguous. On the one hand it relativizes everything it touches, including all interpretations, all memories, all the so-called 'facts'; the implication is, if it is not true, it is 'false,' thus of no value. But since we can never know whether it is 'true' or not, there is no alternative other than to live with the ontological relativism. We make the most of it by our power of imagination, as expressed in the following passage: "Perhaps all of that only takes place in my mind, perhaps it is so that we live only in the illusion of doing this or that, perhaps we carry things out only in our minds, I say, possibly we live only by virtue of our power of imagination that we have cultivated and applied for decades" (5, 25). Rather than precluding meaning, the uncertainty allows meaning to arise. Thus even the 'delusion' takes on meaning: "My oval delusion, ovally-drawn head" (41), which derives perhaps from "my small oval table, Orly table" (54).

Yet that too is subject to revision. The text offers a quotation and extends its metaphorical range: "('undressed and uncoated,' preferably the naked truth)" (57). The 'source' of that quotation is cited later, and it is apparently this very text itself. In its unqualified form, however, an assertion of "the naked truth" can only be meant ironically, together with a string of other platitudes: "I write my books as I have to write them, I call, undressed and uncoated: the naked truth!, but it was a difficult course, but there are no more excuses, form and content condition each other, etcetera" (77). The qualifying adverb of 'preference' is thereby replaced by the equivalence relationship of a colon: "undressed and uncoated: the naked truth!" The text thus relativizes—and mocks—its own efforts at finding the 'truth.' Rather than conceding to the sentimentality of wishing an impossibility, it recognizes the nostalgic appeal of "the naked truth" but also the necessity of renouncing the desire. If truth is inaccessible in any case, it can be presented only as vision; and only in myth are vision and reality one. The fact that authentication takes place on that level perhaps indicates that myth is all we have, and that it is thus synonymous with so-called 'truth.'

The renunciation of any notion of primordial truth behind the memories or of original identity behind the masks liberates the imagination; or, said the other way around, the text willingly admits that the 'essence' was fabricated from alien forms: "One fingers I mean feigns a story, thus one fabricates it" (3, 69)—with the implication, 'not only this story, but every story, also the one that you tell is fingered, feigned, and fabricated.' Just after the assertion, "the story doesn't exist anymore" (59), and before the repetition of that statement (61), an incident is reported that happened at a social gathering (59). The 'story' is totally meaningless, it has no recurring manifestations but constitutes rather simply a dead end. It is "death time" (59), and the narrator registers "a terrible weariness of life" (59). The question of a 'story' is again topicalized and an alternative suggested: "The story doesn't exist anymore. . . the strife-torn feelings, the gestures that have set in resort to repetitive mechanisms, hypnotic cycle, a principle of repetition culled from life" (61). Meaning never coincides with an event; the apparent singularity of the event is rather merely a disguise of repetition.

That must also be part of the narrator's polemic against 'action,' as expressed in a statement stronger than would be necessary simply to justify the narrative form: "I'd like to be relieved of acting, or: I'd like to be relieved of any action, or: I'd like to forestall any attempt at action, or: I'd like to avoid any acting and any action. . . I'm hardly capable of acting and I'm hardly capable of allowing an action, I don't like to act and

I don't like to read anything that has action, thus neither do I write anything that has action or could suggest it" (16, 36). One possible interpretation would be to understand 'action' in the sense of 'over-determination'; an event so complete that nothing remains to be said or done; a fixity of any kind that would prevent further change and thus result in closure. In a process view, such as presented in the text, life and art are regarded as dynamic movement; immobility is inimical to development, and arrestment is tantamount to death. Indeterminacy is achieved by open-ended structures that intentionally display unresolved tension and thus promote further change. Meaning inheres in the repercussions and the succession of links, not in the fact of an action itself. By virtue of reduplication, an experience can be both empirical and imaginative.

There is only one exception to that, only one 'event' that precludes interpretation because 'meaning' coincides with the event. That is the "untimely cutting off" (79). Death, as a "cutting off," is a motif that had been present all along, but 'of course' one does not deal with it until "it becomes imminent" (19). An "eye injury" was reported early on (18, 70), as "(I) almost tore out my eyes" (7). The problem is tracked by the 'bandage' motif (52, 56), and its 'resolution' is narrated in a tone of black humor: "The bandage was gone, but so was the eye" (70). A version of the primeval scream is presented, "as Kleist is supposed to have said upon viewing a painting by Caspar David Friedrich. . . as if a person's eyes were cut out" (47).

It is the limbs of the body, and particularly the arms, that seem most subject to a 'cutting off': "It is the dusk (the demon), the cutting off. . . unfastening the arms the legs" (73, 54; cf. 55, 57). Secondary manifestations include "cutting axils on the buds of plants" (53), "the amputated arms of the tree" (63), and the 'scissors' motif (47, 71, 79). Several times throughout the text, "my arm got into an odd twisted position" (47, 69, 73), presumably from using it as a prop while reading in bed, although another occasion is also mentioned: "when he drew me to him" (69). The discomfort turns into dismemberment, as the speaker realizes the source of the agony, with explicit reference to the lover and implicit reference to the father: "His departure left me in a maimed condition, as if one had removed my arms and legs, namely the Three Kings" (74). The 'weights,' as previously discussed, led to paralysis and loss of limbs. The reference to biblical figures suggests that perhaps the literary form is biblical as well, as the repetitions culminate in a type of 'parable' (71).

Aging entails a loss of physical powers, but it represents also a potential loss of poetic powers. That is denied early in the text: "What Polly claimed recently was totally untrue, namely that fantasy and potency diminish after the age of fifty, precisely the opposite, besides the fact that the power of association increases rather than decreases with increasing age" (19). Thus the narrator's obsession with "the decline of words" (16) seemed initially to be simply another metaphor for a natural phenomenon: "a decline of the moon, a decline of words" (58, 48) or "the decline of words, the decline of the sun" (53). But the narrator has aged through the experience: "Everything has lost some of its effect" (44), and "(I) must artificially generate my own emotions sometimes, they often seem not to be genuinely present anymore" (72). Elements of nature "rehearse the final break-away" (67); but an initial hope that "the memory of this image would consolingly accompany me away when it becomes imminent" (19) seems to break down: "when the great pain comes I'll leave that point" (68). The self—both the writerly self and the personal self—are eminently implicated in the process portrayed.

What remains is a "shadow figure" (16, 10, 12). It had unobtrusively been there all along, like "shadows dipped in paint, shadows of great density, or the colors remained alive in the shadows" (74, 56). It comes to be "one of those wretched (tortured) shadowy figures" of Goya (34, 35). The lover is implicated too, and "through the course of time. . . gradually I saw us in my mind's eye as in fact only pale elongated shadows passing by" (42). Those are the 'shades,' the spirits of the dead in the underworld. At the end "(I) am like the moon and chosen, a bird that sits on the edge and waits, and I don't know whether it means me or only my shadow" (80). The image anticipates—or had been anticipated by—the graveyard experience: "We. . . sit down in the cemetery then presumably in front of our common grave. . . the leafy trees. . . cast their shadows on the gravel path mixed with needles, shaky arabesque-like shadows" (31). Biological and poetic origins are merged under the sign of death, since "Goya, the most transitory, was perhaps my father" (69). The book is thus a poem about transitoriness, a twentieth- (or twenty-first!) century rendition of Shakespeare's "When in the chronicle of wasted time" (*Sonnet* 106) or Goethe's "Ihr naht euch wieder, schwankende Gestalten" (*Faust*, "Once more you near me, wavering apparitions"). Unlike its predecessors, however, there is no claim to immortality, neither for poetry nor for humanity. A Shakespearean bid for immortality on the basis of art, "You still shall live, such virtue hath my pen" (*Sonnet* 81), is unthinkable in a Mayröcker work, despite her emphasis on the writing process. Goethe's *"Ewig-Weibliche"* ("Eternal Feminine") is hardly available to a female poet, but neither does she resort to a simple reversal of gender specification. The closest she comes is the presentation of the father/lover as a 'Christ figure,' who is however portrayed as a 'burial woman.' Perhaps that is one reason for the introduction of androgyny at that point, and the figure in any case remains ambiguous enough to preclude transcendence.

The closest analogy to the Mayröcker text is perhaps Homer's depiction of Hades in the *Odyssey*; but that is only alluded to by means of the 'shadows.' The text is open-ended and seems to suggest that it is the process of life itself that is of value.

v

Perhaps that is part of the 'message' for which the speaker is searching throughout: "I always felt I had to be in search of something but I didn't know what it was" (15, 10, 65, 66). The object of the 'search' is grounded in the natural sphere, for example, in vegetable life: "What did the evergreen trees want to tell me?" (11); or in animal life: "I wished someone would turn my head or my gaze around, like that of an innocent lamb or calf, so it would become aware of specific things, the subjugated submissive human animal, so it would learn to see and hear and become enlightened in mind, sight, and hearing" (75). Those are presumably the "little colored milking animals" referred to earlier (36), or the "feeding as with animals" (40).

The speaker is highly aware of the inadequacy of conventional modes of discourse: "Mere description does not do it, here is a different style" (25, 63). The speaker thus turns to the natural sphere for alternative forms of communication; and the 'zebra' passage mentioned earlier is quoted here in full:

It was an important experience for me, I said, the animal stood there, didn't move, looked deep into my eyes. Later it chased around a bit in its enclosure, but it seemed to me as if it occurred in a dream of the animal, it chased around a bit, but so unreal, so on the borders of its consciousness that I had to cry. It seemed to want to reveal some sort of secret, a message that didn't reach me, I mean there wasn't much of a gap, but then in the last minute I couldn't understand it after all. That message, which I apparently lacked the prerequisites for deciphering, occupied me a long time, did not let me rest for a long time (62).

That the 'message' is not accessible to rational thought elicits a strong reaction on the part of the speaker, and the text continues as follows:

In a strong and angry expression of pain I scream everything into myself without uttering even the slightest sound, a muddled role distribution (62).

The passage leads directly into "a different style":

upon emotional stimulation I try to endure this parrot language, in his letter to the Corinthians Paul said SPEAKING IN TONGUES IS NOT A RATIONAL WAY OF SPEAKING, and he was taken to be mad etcetera (62).

Since rational thought and language had reached their limits, the speaker seeks "a different style." The biblical "speaking in tongues" stands as a metaphor for an alternative to rationality. The author thus appropriates a religious idiom for designating an aesthetic expression of the subconcsious.

In sardonic disinterest in the "gift of gab," which the speaker in any case professes to lack, and in ironic rejection of the Prompter's practical advice, the speaker seeks a new mode of expression. Since "there is no style in which the sought-for object could be presented" (69), one must seek further, as announced seemingly inconsequentially at the beginning of the text: "It's a matter of color, it's a matter of tongue. . . it's a matter of the new color, it's a matter of the new tongue, the new look" (4). That desideratum is communicated by "the ara/parrot in the pet shop with zebra stripes on its chest, with a knowing look, it looked at me a long time" (4). The vacuous old "parrot language" is thus 'endured' because it is leads to the mysterious new 'zebra language.'

The 'message' of the 'zebra language,' however, like the riddle of the Sphinx, remains elusive; or it had remained so from Oedipus until McLuhan, who maintained that 'the medium is the message.' The topicalization of modes of communication, as previously mentioned, refers certainly also to the text itself; and if "pneumatic dispatch" seems a bit arcane, what is more common than the telephone, the "phone booth embushed by green" (63, 75). The image is perhaps a reference to the father, since he had been associated with 'green' from the boughs at the gravesite: "it echoes in me colored green to an extent" (31). It perhaps refers to the lover as well, for "I. . . can also see the NATURAL IMAGE of your figure, bordered by green" (53). The 'phone booth' possibly identifies the father as a 'signal giver' or the 'transmitter' of a 'message,' as previously discussed. Father and lover are again brought together as players in the transmission of meanings.

The speaker too would like to communicate: "I often feel the need to tell someone about my mental fantasies, to inspire someone with them" (21). That constitutes a commitment to communicative discourse. But a disclaimer expresses the writer's doubts about the effectiveness of literature, of this type of literature anyway: "That is the whole world: involuntary signal givers. . . whereas I myself cannot. . . cannot be helpful to anyone as a signal giver, in any case I can't imagine it" (55). The basis for rejection of conventional forms of communication is revealed: "I've always been. . . the opposite of a competent self-salesman, even what I possessed in abundance I could never give thus communicate to anyone else. . . I've always made the biggest detours, not only in art but also in becoming a human being. . . because I've always felt myself so outside the world. . . outside all clouds" (14).

That provides a rationale for the present text to the extent it is "a bit outside the norm, thus unkempt, toward the rakish— wild" (57). Art must sabotage its own best efforts, because it cannot both manifest the ideal and illustrate our distance from it except by deliberately ruining it. There is constant reference

to the inadequacy of language, and language seems to contain its
own erasure: "The felt pens ran out. . . big blots with jagged
edges have flooded everything, ruined all my notes" (7, 12);
"I've also lost the ability to write by hand" (20); "those scribblings in my notebook, those ingenious ideas. . . which I can't
even decipher when I find them again after a few days" (20); "I
woke up with a letter to you. . . had trouble writing it down
however as usual" (53); "there were two lines from a poem by
Poe to be read at the lower edge. . . but I didn't remember
them upon awakening" (61).

Is that not simply a reintroduction of the theological tenet
of the sacred origin of the Word? Is it not a reinscription of
the Romantic notion of metaphysical meaning? Is it not a trans-
position into transcendental terms of a belief in art as a re-
deeming supplement to the limitations of empirical reality? The
answer is, I believe, an emphatic negative; and to see the difference one must consider the view of language presented in
the text.

Speaking or writing so as not to die is undoubtedly as old
as language itself. The fictive speech that borders death is also
poised against it; and to stop the death that would stop it,
language turns back upon itself, doubling itself to become its
own mirror. Writing refers then not to the outside but to
language itself; it divides itself to tell its own story in an
infinite series of duplications. The process is much like the
'doubling' of the self through which the poet projects parts of
the self onto the outside world. On the outside it serves as a
mirror, and the self finds itself as poetic vision, as previously
discussed. Analogously, language divides to find itself in the
refraction, which in turn creates an infinite space where doubles
reverberate. Language thus 'confiscates' what it had posited, just
as the self 'appropriates' what it had projected.

The two parts of the process are inseparable: (1) a naming
of that which lies at the limit of what can be said, and (2) an
inverted repetition of what has already been said. The first is
illustrated by the kind of 'naming' that invests the subject
matter with meaning, which is one possible interpretation of the
phrase, "name comes in to the nonpossessions" (11, 30). The
second is illustrated by the narratorial 'confession' (in heavy
quotation marks), "I repeated, only repeated things" (72). Repe-

tition ironizes, undermines, and empties out the imagery it recycles, stressing its metalingual character as quotation rather than its semantic reference. The language of repetition gives up the power of signification which would subordinate language to thought. The repetition could continue indefinitely, perhaps in a murmuring reminiscent of a Beckett novel. In fact, Beckett's "Unnamable" claims that he is a parrot; and if that is one possible source for the present work, it only illustrates the affinity of the two writers. Mayröcker's recent book *Stilleben* (1991, Still Life) features a figure named "Samuel," who to some extent represents the views of the writer Samuel Beckett. "We want a new style, calls Samuel, we don't want fullness anymore, we want emptiness." If art aspires to be the single, brief, comprehensive cry of a person caught at the moment of death; and if all expression that is not this piercing summation is too trivial to bother with; there is a kind of prolonged discourse that can be derived from apologies for the failure of expression. The postironic evasion of the obligation to express bears witness to the significance of what it evades. That, however, is primarily a later development in Mayröcker's oeuvre, only the beginnings of which are apparent in *Night Train*.

The "principle of repetition" is, however, even in this work not simply a psychological mechanism for problem-solving, nor merely an epistemological test of truth-value. It is, rather, a linguistic means of opening an ontological space where language indefinitely postpones death by indefinitely generating an analogue of itself. Language is 'superimposed' on itself, like the images it presents; and it is at once ironic and naive, both excessive and deficient. The conflict between the duplication of meaning and the duplication of absence results in the ambiguity that pervades the entire work. Difference arises when language can only partially present that which had been present previously but which time has rendered absent. A-categorial thought abandons any organizing principle and writes from a multiplicity that has no center: "I refrain from all considerations and work independently of all demands of social norms and presuppositions" (78). By allowing difference to arise, language escapes the domination of identity and makes visible the discontinuities. It thus creates a space for the operation of truth and falsity.

"Lots of things happen to a person in the process, I mean one has no other choice, but one also wants it that way" (77).

The narrator states facetiously toward the end, "I've become reasonable like a monkey" (72). That is presumably one of the creatures that had been there from the beginning: "I know the little monkey is waiting outside, fluffs up its coat, the little screech owl sat on the door mat and waited for me to let it in" (8, 22). One thinks of Kafka's creatures, particularly since the narrator had earlier revealed, "I read a lot of Kafka" (11). The protagonist in Kafka's "Ein Bericht für eine Akademie" ("A Report for an Academy") tells of his five-year development from monkey to human being. In Kafka or in Mayröcker, the narrator's self-characterization is neither a defense of nor an apology for the text. It has rather the more important effect of authenticating its mode of existence, as evident also in the previously cited self-characterization, "I've always felt myself so outside the world." And authenticity must certainly be part of the 'truth,' to the extent it is accessible to human beings.

* * *

The text poses the question: "How does one's heart establish connections?" (75, 79); and it seems to offer an answer: "The streams of attachment flow under the most disparate things" (67, 79). There are many more associations than could be suggested here and undoubtedly more that I have not thought of. The reader is invited to join in the process, since, as said earlier, "every network of thoughts immediately wants to be spun out further, and other high-flying landscapes." That 'network,' which entails "constant correction of course" and thus includes "crossed-out passages for example" (65, 35, 41, 77), could be visualized as a mobile, a series of concentric circles or spirals, rotating around a mysterious center. Presentation of the contents of consciousness in that way illustrates the utter impossibility of defining or delimiting the coordinates in which the mind moves.

A knowledge of the whole is essential to an understanding of any of its parts, and thus, as has also been said of Joyce's writings, a work cannot be read but can only be re-read, each time subject to revision. The book can profitably be read both forwards and backwards, perhaps starting in the middle. (The experiment recommends itself, especially since the present analysis is not intended to 'domesticate' the text or to impose on it an order, the very existence of which is radically refuted by the being of the text. At best, the analysis picks up on a mode of reading suggested by the text itself for 'spinning out' a "network of thought.")

The question remains to what extent the work may be regarded as autobiographical; that is, what is the relationship between literature and life? In that the work takes the self as its subject, it may be regarded as a type of 'autobiography'; but the centrality of the writing process leads one to view it as creating the self it portrays, for this type of literature is as formative as it is reproductive. Recognizable features from the author's empirical life are included, but they provide only the surface props. Real-life elements are so transformed that rather than any 'confessional,' the text represents a recovery of the self's own history in terms of a fictional documentation of the creative process, which is itself a series of imaginative events.

The 'sea-change' that the self thereby undergoes is so thorough that at times the text seems to produce the author rather than the author the text. The narrator appears not as a manipulator of metaphors but as an accomplice in a dynamic relation to them, reacting momentarily to the gradual disclosure of the fuller significance of the controlling images. But of course the author produces both—the text and thereby also the artist-self, as well as the other figures and the natural elements. That is neither an imperialistic gesture nor one of self-sufficiency; too much has been said to allow any such notions to arise. It is rather part of the utopian vision of unity, the *todo* that causes its opposite, the *nada*, to be felt so poignantly. Whatever else the book may be about, it represents an exploration of the nature and consequences of commitment to poetic vision, 'poetic' again as synonymous with 'existential.'

Since the process as well as the product is fictionalized, the question reverts to the relationship between real-life talking about (the process of) art and the fictional (product of) art itself. The two are shown to be inextricably intertwined; indeed, each takes the other as its presupposition, since the product portrays the process that creates the product. That type of cause-and-effect relationship is expressed in ordinary language by the metaphor of 'chicken-and-egg,' which is one possible interpretation of a textual passage: "Spooning honey from the jar, at the breakfast table, smell and taste of chicken and egg" (72). If that relationship is one of complete recursivity, it only demonstrates the extent to which existence takes itself as its own presupposition. We know the myth, not the truth—unless the myth itself is true.

If the work is enigmatic, as readers have often found Mayröcker's works to be, it is a purposive enigma. Writing in an epistemologically decentered mode reminds one that all meaning is constructed intersubjectively, that is, in the space between writer and reader. Art is experience—certainly for the creator, but also for the receiver, who is an accomplice in the discovery and invention of meanings. If a reader occasionally loses his or her bearings in a text, that is not so different from his or her encounters in the world. If "life has become too extensive to allow for an overview," the text may be seen as a mimetic replication of that state of affairs. The artist's response is to exploit the uncertainty of the situation as a source of creative strength. The intensity of the experience may well lead the participants—both writer and reader—to say at the end with Brecht, "The chaos is behind us; the good times are over."

Reality inheres not in a counterfeit integration of life but in a scattering of random souvenirs whose charm derives from the inviting spaces between them: "cracks in reality, the view of the holy proportions behind it" (22). To strive for full comprehension or to search for fixed meanings would be to insist on a totality and finality that do not exist. With that recognition—the result of a metaphorical journey through a real Hades—the book closes open-endedly by convincingly conjuring up the new morning, "The good day. . . " (80).

* * * * *

ENVOI: I would like personally and publicly to thank Friederike Mayröcker for her help with the translation and her patience in going through the entire text with me. Gratitude is due also to Ernst Jandl for his invaluable assistance. (It goes without saying that errors and misunderstandings are my own responsibility.) The book is dedicated to F. Mayröcker Sr.

Beth Bjorklund

ABOUT THE BOOK

"Friederike Mayröcker presents her readers with many puzzles; but among the numerous, currently inflationary topics of auto-biographical prose, her work crystallizes the central issues."

Frankfurter Allgemeine Zeitung, Frankfurt

"*Night Train* portrays a dangerous trip that the self, at once timorous and bold, somnambulistically undertakes through the unconscious."

Neue Zürcher Zeitung, Zurich

"How does it happen that we are so gripped by this book? Is it perhaps because the seemingly specific problems presented here constitute our basic human concerns?"

Die Presse, Vienna

"Just as the text defies description, so also does it serve as an indication of future possibilities for poetry. Anyone who is drawn into the tow of the book will continue to write it for him-or herself."

Lesezirkel, Vienna

"The text is unsettling in many ways, yet the reader must marvel at the absolute resolve with which Mayröcker pursues her journey of self-discovery."

World Literature Today, USA